Trailing the wrong thug can be dangerous!

But Johnny Marshall knew this was the right man, because if anybody looked like a mobster's gorilla, Bat Wiley did.

As Johnny watched, Bat stepped into the long black car. Then he slipped into the stream of traffic. Johnny took off after him and pulled alongside just as the intersection lights turned red.

But when he glanced over at the big black car, there was no sign of the gorilla—only a pimply-faced kid giving Johnny the once-over.

Worse still, the gun in the kid's hand—its round muzzle gazing coldly through the window like a hit man's third eye—was pointing straight at Johnny.

James M. Fox

is also the author
of Raven House Mystery #33

The Wheel Is Fixed

He was in trouble—real trouble. And
there was no way out!

Richard Bailey was a very good
bandleader. He was also a very bad
gambler…and he owed a lot of
money to the mob. He had no way of
paying them off, so they made him an
offer he couldn't refuse.

It looked like a very sweet setup—but
it was really a setup for death!

A SHROUD
FOR
MR. BUNDY

James M. Fox

A RAVEN HOUSE MYSTERY FROM
W🌐RLDWIDE
TORONTO · LONDON · NEW YORK

First Printing February 1981

ISBN 0-373-60045-3

Printed in Canada

1

THE SHABBY LITTLE MAN said formally, without a stutter or a hiccup, "How d'you do? I'm Jeremiah Peter Bundy, and I'm dead." He nodded solemnly to the assembled company as if to make quite sure we'd understand, and promptly collapsed on the lawn, and started vomiting into the freshly watered basin of my avocado tree.

We looked at him, and at each other, with a mixture of annoyance and considerable startled curiosity. Mary Brownell laid down her bridge hand, fumbled in her silver-mesh-brocaded evening bag for cigarettes, and frowned on me in sociable disapproval, as if she had caught me with a button off my shirt. Her husband coughed irascibly and jammed the stub of his cigar right back between his teeth. Mrs. Suzanne Willet Marshall winked at me and kicked my ankle rather sharply under cover of the green suede-lined tabletop. Khan, our Great Dane, rose languidly from where he had been snoring on the patio tiles, and padded over to investigate. He sniffed at the intruder's trouser legs and backed away a step or two, his tawny hide bunching in ripples of disgust. The growl that came up from his belly sounded puzzled and disturbed.

I glanced a trifle wistfully at the three aces and some half a dozen kings and queens I had just dealt myself, and stacked them up in front of me, and grudgingly pushed back my chair. It was the sort of thing you could expect on such a night as this—a January night in southern California, with the thermometer at ninety degrees from a desert heat wave, and the city taken over by the Honorable and Exalted Order of the Knights of Araby, assembled in their yearly rampage somewhat euphemistically advertised as a Grand Divan and Conclave. Our place in Brentwood, north of Sunset, was a little off the beaten track, a quietly residential neighborhood for university professors, movie-studio technicians and the like, but for two days we'd seen the stragglers drifting by, and on the boulevard the purple turban and the bedsheet-white burnoose were crowding out the rainbow sport shirt and the imitation Panama.

The little man had gone to sleep. He'd pulled his knees up under him and dug his nose into my newly mown dichondra patch. His breath was regular, if rather noisy, and as aromatic as a working still. I slapped the dog away from him and turned him over with one foot. I'd have enjoyed the application of a polished Oxford on a more strategic spot than just his shoulder, for the incident was pretty inconveniently timed. My guests' approval was important to me—Frank Brownell happened to be the district manager for Mutual Indemnity of Boston, which supplied my only regular retainer at the time.

"Wake up, Jack," I said coldly. "Turn it off. You're missing all the fun downtown."

The porch light caught his face and made him out in his late fifties, hatless, almost bald, with stringy fringes of gray-peppered hair behind the ears. He had the bottle baby's coarsely grained complexion, and his little mouth hung slack, disclosing two gold crowns and a half-dozen plugs in what was otherwise a fairly well-preserved array of rabbit teeth. The straggly bristle of his mustache seemed to be infested with a lot of dandruff flakes.

I grabbed his ankles, jerked his legs to shake him up. Behind me, Frank Brownell produced a noise somewhere between a horse laugh and a growl. "Why not just dump it back into the gutter?" he inquired impatiently.

"There isn't any on this street," I said. "And if a car comes by and knocks him off, I'd be responsible." The little man had lost his wallet when I turned him over, so I picked it up. The worn old pigskin held about three hundred bucks in cash, a half-used book of stamps, two ragged clippings from a crossword-puzzle magazine and something like a dozen cards proclaiming membership of J.P. Bundy of Racine, Wisconsin, in the Farm Equipment Dealers of America, the Lions Club, the Mishiwaka Men's Athletic League, the Sigma Phi Alumni Association of Wisconsin University, and so on down the list.

I said over my shoulder, "Guess he can afford a cab. We'd better get him one."

Mary Brownell said coolly, "If the driver won't object...."

Her husband snorted, struck a match to benefit his dead cigar, pushed back his chair and wandered over to inspect the evidence. "Some cab ride!" he suggested sourly. "Fifteen hundred miles!"

The carefully streamlined young woman with the gleaming auburn curls who'd shared my bed and board for almost thirteen years came through the

French doors from the den and crossed the patio to
us in long-legged, graceful strides. "Johnny, we're
stuck with him for twenty minutes, I'm afraid," she
said.

"How's that?"

"I've talked with the dispatcher, darling. All his
cabs are busy with convention passengers. He'll
send us one as soon as it calls in." She slipped a vial
from the first-aid kit into my hand.

The knife-edged pungence of ammonia cut
through the sultry night scents of jasmine and
lemon blossoms. Frank Brownell backed hastily
away and swore at me under his breath. Our visitor
convulsively pulled up his knees and sneezed. His
eyelids twitched until he clapped them shut again
with both his little hands. He started talking in a
preacher's hollow baritone, its somber intonation
only slightly marred by a Midwestern twang. "Man
that is born of woman is of but few days, and full of
trouble," he declared.

I touched his shoulder, but he shook me off and
slowly sat up on the lawn. "He shall come to his
grave in a full age, like as a shock of corn cometh in
season," he informed us solemnly. "So it must be
that we are gathered here in sorrow, mourning the
departure of our well-beloved kinsman, friend and
brother in the Lord, whose name was Jeremiah
Peter Bundy...." Suddenly he winced and let his
hands fall by his side. His eyes were open, looking
at us, rather startled but entirely sober now. "I beg
your pardon," he said in a very normal tone of
voice. "I fear I've had too much to drink."

It probably was funny, but nobody seemed to be
amused. I put the stopper on the vial of ammonia
and tossed his wallet in his lap. Suzy said thought-

fully, "You mustn't do that, Mr. Bundy. Not out here in Hollywood. It's very dangerous, unless someone is with you to take care of you. Your family is probably already worried sick."

The stare he gave her, peering up at her from where he was still squatting on the grass, was soberly, politely puzzled. "But I haven't any family," he said. "That's why.... You see, they buried me this afternoon. At Shady Dell Memorial Park."

We stared right back at him, and even Frank Brownell kept quiet somehow. Our visitor did not appear at all disturbed by this collective diffidence. He poked into his wallet, fished the crossword clippings out and checked a penciled note that had escaped me on the back of one of them. "Could you direct me to 6130 North Broxton, please?" he asked us anxiously.

Suzy reached out to touch my arm and caught her breath. I felt my grin set in suspicious disbelief. "Sure, this is it," I said. "What's on your mind, my friend?"

That seemed to bother him. He blinked at me uncertainly and said, "Are you...?" and staggered to his feet. He'd more or less caught up with things, but from his point of view the picture with four people and a dog in it, grouped sociably on a California garden patio just didn't look quite right. "I tried the classified directory," he hesitatingly confessed. "There were a lot of places listed near to my hotel, but most of them in office buildings had already closed. The only one that was still open was where they just laughed at me and didn't understand."

I winked at Frank Brownell, whose scowl of irritation almost swallowed his cigar, and said, "Oh, didn't they? What's your hotel?"

"The Arizona Palms. You see, I've recently re-tired from business, and this is my first trip out west in fifteen years."

"Well, Mr. Bundy, that's all right. I'm sure the west is proud to have you. Now if you'll just relax, your cab will be here pretty soon and we can all of us take up where we left off."

He pinched his little gray mustache, releasing dandruff by the ounce. "My cab? I couldn't get a cab; I had to walk. It seemed quite far."

We stared at him some more. He'd walked five miles on nothing but a skinful of bad whiskey in a town where even postmen come on wheels. "Why did you do that, Mr. Bundy?" Suzy asked him care-fully.

"Because I want to *know*." He sounded very earnest and sincere about it, as if nothing else could ever matter to him anymore. "I want you people to *investigate*."

Mary Brownell produced a nervous giggle, as if she'd found out about the way I usually got my cus-tomers. Her husband wasn't scowling anymore—he seemed to be bemused in studying our visitor with something of a bill collector's interest in rubber checks. "Exactly what is this you thought to have investigated, Mr. Bundy?" I inquired.

"I want you to discover for me what occurred this afternoon." He almost said *dishcover*, but he caught himself in time and saved his dignity with a slight stutter. "The experience I had has left me somewhat c-confused. You see, I had a rather heavy lunch at the Brown Derby, and decided on a little constitutional to keep myself in trim. It wasn't very long before I found myself in what I then presumed to be a public park. There was a little lake with swans in it, and near its shore a rather large and handsome building with its entrance under a marquee. I took this building for a c-café, but when I went inside there was a very sympathetic lady there behind a desk who asked me if I wanted to attend the Bundy services. I was surprised, of course, and couldn't think of anything to say, and she conducted me into another room with many people, and a c-c-coffin on a bier, and flowers, and a minister who frowned at me when I came in. He had just started speaking, and it took awhile before I realized that he was speaking about *me*.''

I pursed my lips and Suzy said, ''Oh, no! What did you do?''

''At first,'' the little man said earnestly, ''I told myself it had to be the heat. There were some benches in the park, and I was sure I must have gone to sleep on one of them. I p-p-pinched myself, like this.'' He showed us where, and just how hard. ''It was no dream,'' he solemnly assured us. ''I was wide awake, and it was me they meant to bury in that coffin. So of course I sneaked away, as soon as nobody was looking at me anymore.''

Mary Brownell obliged with one more nervous giggle. Suzy smiled at her politely. ''But it doesn't really *mean* much, does it?'' she protested. ''Even if you were a bit upset at first, you must have realized that Bundy isn't such a terribly uncommon name.''

I couldn't manage any better than a patient lack of interest. I thought it was a pretty piece of quaint coincidence, if true, but I had never come across a bottle baby who could tell a story straight. Most of them hardly even know what's going on. ''Well, after all,'' I said, ''he took this mortuary for a bar.''

The little man looked hurt. He was still worrying his mustache, and the dandruff was still coming down like snow in Canada. "You don't b-b-believe me," he accused us, almost tearfully.

"Why not?" I said.

"Of course we do," said Suzy. "But we don't agree there's anything for you to fret about. You should go home and get a good night's sleep, and in the morning you'll feel better, Mr. Bundy. You don't want to waste your money hiring anybody to investigate a stranger's funeral."

As if on cue, a Yellow cab came idling down the hill and pulled into our driveway with a squeal of brakes. The dog jumped to his feet and barked at it, then caught himself and slumped back on the patio, his watchful sulphur-yellow eyes once more unblinkingly fixed on our visitor. The little man did not appear to notice him. His shoulders sagged dejectedly; he turned away and started stumbling off across the lawn.

"Hey, just a minute, you!" snapped Frank Brownell through his cigar.

I stared at him. The little man stopped in his tracks and waited, swaying slightly in the breeze that wasn't there. He did not seem to trust himself to look around. "You wanted an investigation, didn't you?" Frank asked him silkily. "That's what you came out here for, walking all the way? Why give up now?"

This time the little man glanced back over his shoulder in disturbed bewilderment. "You mean you'll d-d-do it?" he demanded haltingly.

"I'm not a private dick," Frank told him smugly. "Mr. Marshall is. He didn't say he wouldn't take your case."

There were a couple of expressions admirably fitting the occasion in the use of which the Army had instructed me ten years before. I swallowed them and blinked a little with the effort. "Yeah, that's right. I didn't say."

"Sure thing you didn't," Frank said heartily. He slapped me on the shoulder like a wayward older brother getting set to sell me a remarkable investment opportunity.

"Oh, Johnny, *honestly*," said Suzy, but our visitor was already fumbling for his wallet, eagerly. "How m-m-much?" he asked me, looking up at me with red-rimmed, liquidly expectant little eyes.

"Oh, that," I said. "Well, yeah, if you insist, I guess a hundred dollars ought to cover it." He pushed a bill into my hand before I had a chance to reach for it. The cabbie in the driveway touched his horn. "Want me to give you a receipt?"

"That won't be n-n-necessary, sir." It sounded just as if he'd bought himself a sudden dignity. "I only want to *know*. When may I count on your r-r-report?"

"Sometime tomorrow morning, I suppose," I said. "By lunchtime, anyway. I'll get in touch with you at your hotel. Are you quite sure you don't have any relatives in town?"

The taxi driver honked again, impatiently. "Oh, yes," my brand-new client promised me. "Quite sure. You see, I am of old Alsatian farmer stock. My father came to W-Wisconsin back in twenty-one and married late in life. He and my mother p-p-passed away while I was still a child." Now that he'd paid his money and had gained my ear, he seemed inclined to make the most of it.

I put my arm through his and marched him off

across the lawn. He meekly came along and let me bundle him into the cab. "You'll call me in the m-m-morning, sir?" he urged me, clinging to my hand with both of his. "I only want to *know*...."

The driver raced his motor, watching us with wearily concealed asperity. "Let's go, pal," he suggested crossly. "Lots of other people need this transportation, see?" He spat into my second rosebush from the left and slammed his gears, backed out and grumbled down the hill.

I strolled back to the patio and dropped into my chair. Suzy gave me a second cup of coffee and a puzzledly bewitching smile. Mary Brownell fitted another cigarette into her holder and leaned forward decorously to accept my lighter flame. "Such interesting lives you two must lead," she murmured between puffs.

Her husband seemed to be absorbed in studying his bridge hand. I picked up my own and started sorting it, a trifle absentmindedly. "Frank sees to it we do," I said.

"Well, what about it?" snapped that worthy gentleman. "Aren't you in business to make a buck, the same as everybody else?"

"I'm in the business of finding facts," I said. "The kind of facts a client couldn't find himself, or anyway not easily or inexpensively. Tomorrow, when this Bundy character wakes up, he'll realize that all he needs to do is get the Hall of Records on the phone. I was about to tell him that when you stuck in your oar. You knew it, too, so why the switch?"

He chuckled for me, half embarrassedly. "You don't recall the name?"

"It sounds familiar, sure. I must've come across it half a dozen times. What's wrong with it?"

"I guess that was before your time. Six, seven years ago we had some dealings at the office with a fellow, seems to me he even had the same initials: J.P. Bundy, wholesale jewelry. I think the association has a file, but never got enough to lay a squeal on him."

That made a bit of difference, of course, although not very much. What he was telling me amounted to no more than that, at Mutual Indemnity, some jeweler named Bundy had once been suspected as a fence, had been investigated unsuccessfully and turned in to the Casualty Underwriters' National Association, with no further helpful hints coming to light. Frank killed the stub of his cigar, scowled back at me and said, "Okay, so it was just a hunch. It's still your case, and you got paid for it. You play it any way you like."

I shook my head and shrugged. The bridge cards I was holding felt a little sticky from the heat, but they still made the best hand I had seen that evening. We were a thousand points behind, and we could use a hand like that. Then I looked closer, winced and made a barely sociable noise.

The hand I'd dealt myself had fourteen cards.

2

THE SUN WAS MARCHING IN behind a brass band through the kitchen window while I dug into my breakfast eggs. At 9:00 A.M. there was too much of it already to wear anything but shorts. The *Post-Courier* screamed at me all the way across its front page Hot Enough for You? and featured under that a picture of two polar bears perched on a chunk of ice at the Chicago zoo.

The dog lay like a couchant lion on the tiles across the exit to the service porch; a yard of coarse pink tongue drooped from his panting muzzle while he whined insistently at Suzy, who was slicing apples on the drainboard, getting set to bake a pie. She tossed a core to him. He caught it, crunching it with evident enjoyment. "Johnny, are we doing anything today?"

"I've got a lot of paperwork," I said.

Her loosely tied blue housecoat rustled as she swung around; the sun struck sparks of auburn from her sleek long permanent. "You took a case last night."

"Two phone calls ought to handle it."

"It's Saturday," she carefully reminded me.

I grunted in some mild distress. The County Hall of Records would be closed. "Oh, great," I said.

"Well, darling, after all, you promised. For a hundred dollars, don't you think he is entitled to a little service from us?''

"Not from us, he isn't, sugar doll. From me, he is.''

She made a face at me. In my peculiar profession most of us are married, and the women usually help by taking messages, attending to the mail and generally putting up with us—the hard-guy bachelor who pays a giddy office blonde to get him into jams is strictly from TV, of course. Not many of the wives are even interested in the job itself, but mine has always had a bug about it, claiming she knows how, and wanting in.

"Some other time," I said. "This thing is just routine.''

It was a little cooler in the den, but not enough. I set the blinds and, in the semidarkness that resulted, switched the desk lamp on and dropped into my battered swivel chair. There was a pile of notes stacked on the blotter, and the first two paragraphs of a report for Mutual Indemnity on half a dozen local bonding prospects occupied the typewriter beside it on the shelf. I gave myself a cigarette and sat there sweating quietly with my slippered feet up on the desk. The slatted backrest of the swivel chair cut tracks into my unprotected skin. Certain unkindly speculations about Frank Brownell's intelligence and on the subject of his likely ancestry passed casually through my mind.

The telephone directory lay within easy reach. I reached for it and heaved it up into my lap, and ran a sticky finger down the Bundy listings, all eighteen of them. The right initials were not there. That meant exactly nothing in a town where half the population doesn't care to list its phones. I leafed

on through the book and looked up Shady Dell
Memorial Park. It had four numbers, listed ones, and
probably a good deal more than eighteen lines. I
shook my head and heaved the book back on the
desk and yawned without restraint. I didn't want to
do a lick of work. It was the kind of day for driving to
the beach and loafing with a bottle of cold beer. It
was the kind of day for lying in a hammock on the
patio, digging a fork into iced watermelon, if this
were July and watermelon could be had. I called myself a silly name and swung my feet back to the floor
and marched upstairs to climb into some clothes.

Mrs. Suzanne Willet Marshall smiled for me in-
quisitively when I drifted through the kitchen on
my way to the garage. "What time do you want
lunch?"

"Oh, I don't know. I'll wrap this up by noon all
right."

"I've got a hairdresser's appointment at eleven-
thirty," she informed me. "If you want to pick me
up, I'll go by bus and we could eat downtown."

"Don't let him cut too much of it. I like it just
about the way it is."

"But Johnny, it's old-fashioned wearing it this
long."

"That's me," I said. "Old-fashioned. Gaslight,
and long-handled underwear, and crackers in my
soup." She stood on tiptoes, with a saucepan and
a towel in her hands, and I bent down to kiss one
corner of her smiling, claret-luscious lips, and
wandered on across the service porch. The dog had
lumbered to his feet and tried to squeeze outside
with me until I had to throw a shoulder block at him
and slap him down. They disapprove of you out
here if you bring pets into a cemetery.

Shady Dell, of course, is only one of six or seven widely famous southern California charnel grounds. It covers something like a hundred acres of a gently sloping, palm-tree-studded hillside, less than a long rifleshot from Hollywood and Vine. Two large blue dusty Gray Line tour buses were parked beside the open gates; their cargo of some sixty purple-turbaned Knights of Araby was trudging up the winding asphalt road to Statuary Hall. I pulled into the inside parking lot and crossed the greensward to a rambling Georgian structure of red brick and gray cement blocks, with a moss-green gabled roof. A man in khaki overalls was puttering about the lawn, relaxing in the saddle of a tractor mower, neatly clipping six-foot swaths out of the rich Kentucky grass. Two fat old ladies dressed in fashionable black were watching dotingly a little boy in a Lone Ranger outfit galloping along the lakeshore, snapping with both pistols at the lazy-drifting, haughtily oblivious white swans.

The Georgian building's cheerful candy-striped marquee reached out for twenty yards along the graveled walk on painted iron poles. It bore no lettering of any kind, and might conceivably have been mistaken for the avenue of entry to a less sedate establishment. The polished beechwood door surrendered to my finger tips, admitting me into a spacious, air-conditioned lobby carpeted in rose and silver gray. Behind the carved Italian walnut desk a very tall and almost startlingly attractive redhead in a Debutante Shop floral cotton print got up and came to meet me with a rather obviously practiced sympathetic smile.

I asked to see the manager and gave my name. She let the smile fade out and measured me with a less interested, more appraising eye. "Is he expecting you?" She saw me shake my head. "You're not a cosmetologist applying for the vacancy we had? It's filled."

It happens all the time, of course. It gets a little tiresome, but you just can't tell them who you are and what you really want. They get a mental picture of you peeking through hotel-room keyholes, and they freeze on you immediately. "I need some information," I said carefully.

"Of course. Then maybe I can help you, sir."

"It's not your kind of information, honey."

She frowned for me and hesitated, turned away and strode back to the desk to fiddle with her intercom keys. I fished a cigarette out of my pocket, scowled at it and put it back. There were some paintings on the paneled walls, and one of them was "Joseph Counsels Pharaoh," a life-size copy in a vast antique gilt frame, so I strolled over for a look at that. It would have fitted just as nicely in a high-class corporation lawyer's waiting room.

"Excuse me, is there something I can do for you?"

He almost made me jump, and not because he'd managed to sneak up on me. He was a ringer for my Uncle Ralph, who used to run the History department at Cornell while I was going through the motions there. He had the same short chubby body in the same blue double-breasted pinstripe suit, starched Oxford collar and blue regimental tie. The same round moonface, gravely guileless, closely shaved and generously chinned; the same white shock of hair brushed back in military style. But Uncle Ralph's coronary had quit cold on him ten years ago.

"About the Bundy funeral," I said, a little louder than I'd meant to pitch my voice.

He briefly creased his smooth white brow. "This way, sir, if you please."

The door was chastely lettered Family Reception Room. The walls were tempered in a clover-green pastel; the furniture was imitation Chippendale. The pseudofireplace shone with polished brass and had a small electric log. The only picture was a watercolor of Lake Arrowhead above the mantelpiece. A rather large bouquet of tulips graced the flower stand between the windowsills. "Be seated, sir. You represent the press?"

I let myself be waved into a wing chair with a staid Colonial print and introduced myself. He dropped into its mate and faced me with the light behind him. "You may smoke," he told me, and I noticed then my fingers had been twiddling with the same unlighted cigarette. A match appeared from nowhere in his large smooth steady hand, snapped into fire and reached across to me. "I've startled you a bit," he said unsmilingly. "A place like this, no matter how we try.... I'm probably reminding you of some close relative or friend who has been gone for many years. We always do, somehow, in this profession, and particularly so for visitors who come on business and have not suffered any recent loss themselves." He leaned back in his chair and looked at me, politely interested in my problems, comfortably sure of his ability to deal with them.

"There would have been no need to bother you," I said. "But as you know, the coroner's administrative files are closed today."

His brow went up again. "You wish to see the

Bundy death certificate? In whose behalf, sir, if you please?''

"There's no suspicion of irregularities involved," I said. "It's public information, after all.''

"Irregularities! I should hope not.'' He raised his hands in horrified rejection. "Possibly you do not realize that this inquiry you are making of me, sir, is very much irregular itself. Are you a member of the family?''

I made a doubtful effort at impatient arrogance. "Let's try to get there without worrying about exactly what I am or whom I represent. You know the only reason why I'm here. The county clerk won't even need to ask my name.''

"Ah, to be sure. But this is not the office of the county clerk,'' he pointed out. "In any case, I cannot show you the certificate. Our practice is to file them every day by messenger.''

"You've got a burial permit,'' I said. "It states the same essential facts. I'll bet you wouldn't even have to look them up.''

He strung his hands as if in prayer and rested both his smooth round chins on them to stare at the cool gray Axminster rug between his feet. I almost asked him if he'd ever watched while Uncle Ralph explained about the Second Punic War. "We have a policy of not discussing information of this kind, except, of course, with members of the family of the deceased,'' he told me distantly.

"But heavens, man, I only want his previous address, his occupation and the date and cause of death,'' I argued in protest. "It doesn't matter to me where he's buried, or how much you charged for it, or who sent flowers, or what organ music was performed. Just stuff that any citizen has legal

access to, on what they use for working days downtown. I understand you people aren't supposed to
do the county's job. But if you do, it's hardly more
than just a courtesy."

The room fell quiet. It was the kind of brief, un-
comfortable silence bankers take advantage of
before they disapprove of your collateral. The only
sound remaining was a fluttering of ribbons from
the ceiling outlet of the air-conditioning machinery.
A fly rose off the tulips, casually buzzed my nose
and settled slowly on the nearest windowpane. I
twitched a shoulder blade to shed the perspiration
that was getting chilly there.

The mortuary manager unstrung his hands and
dropped them onto his knees. The gesture served
his heavy body in supplying added leverage for getting up. "A business like ours, Mr. Marshall, must
exist by courtesy," he said. "But you will recognize, no doubt, that those whose loved ones we
have laid to rest must have first claim on it. Unless
you care to prove to us that you've been authorized
by Mr. Bundy's relatives to make this most unusual
inquiry, we can only favor them, relying upon our
professional discretion as a policy."

"It's up to you," I said. "Quite frankly, I don't
even know his relatives."

"Just so." His tone made clear he couldn't make
himself believe or understand a word of it. "You
will excuse me now? This is a pretty busy day for
us."

He waddled out behind me, crossed the lobby in
my wake and bowed me ceremoniously out into the
park. I strolled some fifty yards along the graveled
walk, retraced my steps unhurriedly, pushed back
into the lobby, briskly strode up to the desk once

more. The redhead was alone. She did not rise this time; the look she gave me held a mixture of annoyance and of languid curiosity, but not the kind that knew about me and about the flea I carried in my ear.

"Yes, sir. Did you forget something?" Her glance was on the notebook I pretended to consult.

"Just the address," I said. "The doctor's address. Will you check it for me, please?"

"Of course." She swiveled in her high-backed leather chair; one slender, well-groomed hand reached for the drawers of a filing cabinet. This was her chance to show me who could give me information there. "Which one?"

"The Bundy burial. J.P. Bundy. Yesterday's."

She nodded, pulled a drawer, riffled through the cards. "It's 9075 West Cameron, in Beverly."

"That's Dr. Martin Helm?"

"Oh, no. You've got it wrong," she solemnly assured me. "It was Dr. Richard Foreman signed the death certificate. There's nothing here about a Dr. Helm."

"You're right," I said. "My error. Got my signals crossed. Thanks very much. Next time I'll bring a box of candy for you, honey."

On my way out, the brooding eyes of Pharaoh appeared to follow me clear down across the lawn and through the gates.

3

THE BUILDING ON WEST CAMERON was mostly plate glass, structural aluminum and glazed concrete. Its parking lot, with row on serried row of Mercedes 450 SL's, Cadillacs, and Lincoln Continentals, swallowed half the block in rear.

The ground-floor crescent that enclosed the dome-roofed entrance hall was occupied by a prescription pharmacy, all onyx tile and banks of daylight fluorescent tubes and crisp young gentlemen in horn-rimmed spectacles and starched white surgeon's coats, as if to sell you the idea it might be fun to go ahead and catch something. The indicator board between the elevators listed half a hundred names that ended in M.D. The elevator cage that took me up to five was big enough to take a stretcher, and the queasy redolence of hexolin clung faintly to its walls.

There were a lot of people in the cheerful, air-conditioned waiting room. They all looked vaguely under fifty, and they showed a lot of nicely suntanned skin in strapless cotton prints. I ran the rapid crossfire of their frankly speculative glances and approached the glassed-in nurse's desk. The pretty one was furiously typing, with the earpiece of a dictaphone recorder in place. The gray-haired, buxomly maternal one slid back a panel to survey me with a practiced eye. "Good morning, sir. And how are you this lovely morning?"

"Kind of warm," I said, and used a handkerchief on my perspiring brow to prove the point.

"You men are all the same," she chided me. "A gorgeous California winter day like this, and you complain." She briefly studied her appointment book. "I don't believe we have your name."

I grinned and gave it to her, and she promptly started making out a card for me. "Your address, Mr. Marshall, please?"

"I'm not a patient, ma'am."

She raised her eyes and caught the warning shift in mine. At least a dozen shell-like ears had been tuned in on us all through the room, with varying degrees of furtiveness. She smiled for me, a bland, professional smile, and put a pad and pencil on the panel shelf in front of me.

I wrote on it: "*Re J.P. Bundy, family inquiry, urgent,*" gave it back to her and watched her smile, and grabbed the only vacant chair still left before she had a chance to try and pin me down some more. The magazines they had in there ran heavily to *Vogue, Mademoiselle* and *Cosmo,* but the morning paper made a better window screen. Traffic moved pretty steadily along. More rustling skirts, elaborately casual soprano voices, briskly clicking heels, arrived to take the place of those that disappeared into the corridor to the consulting rooms. These days the way to make a living in the medical profession is to keep them coming in and run them through on the assembly line.

The gray-haired nurse was beckoning to me behind the open panel. "Doctor says he'll see you now." She dropped her voice to confidential level

in benign admonishment. "You mustn't keep him.
Doctor's always very busy Saturdays. . . ."

The corridor was rubber-floored, and maple-
paneled to the ceiling plinths. There was a heady
scent of Turkish cigarette smoke, French perfume
and sterilizing alcohol. The open transom of a dressing room gave passage to a low-pitched laugh, half
shrewish, half amused. The pretty nurse who had
been typing at the desk came tripping out and
slammed the door. She almost spilled the towel-
covered tray she carried, bumping into me; the
double take she gave me seemed a little flustered.
"Oh. In there."

"In there" was three doors down and proved to be
a whitewashed cubicle that barely offered space to
one small table, two straight chairs, a bookcase and a
glass-walled cabinet for instruments. The table
served an empty blotter and a telephone; three
inches of the chair behind it furnished desultory
parking space to a young man, exceptionally tall and
lankily constructed, with a thin, pale, clever face,
tired hazel eyes that looked remote and nervously
preoccupied, and a vast rumpled disarray of rich
black hair as wavy as a movie star's. His not-quite-
fresh white coat hung limply open to disclose a
T-shirt and a pair of old gray flannel slacks as he
hunched forward on the blotter, mumbling at the
phone. "Okay, dear. . . . Yeah, I will. How's
that? . . . Sure, I'll remember. . . . Yeah, uh-huh.
You bet. Whose dinner party? . . . Oh, of course.
Well, I dunno. I guess so, if you want to. . . . No, I'm
not. I can't discuss it now. . . . No, dear, uh-uh, it
isn't. Just a man who wants some information. . . .
Sure, that's all. Hello? . . ." He frowned into the
phone and laid it gently back into its cradle,

straightened up and squeezed his jaw with one
long, pale and very steady hand. He looked at me
without much interest. "Excuse me, where were
we? Oh, yes, the Bundy embolism. Certainly. Bad
business, unfortunate indeed. You realize, of
course, there wasn't anything could have been
done to save him or prevent it happening. By me or
anybody else. Allow me to extend my sympathy."

"It was an embolism, then?" I said.

"No doubt about it. None at all. I thought I'd
made that clear." The tired, light-hazel eyes had
sharpened up a bit with irritation. "To Miss Lord, at
least. On Thursday morning when he passed away.
She seemed to understand."

I nodded, vaguely noncommittal, and his glance
turned wistfully impatient as it dropped back to the
phone. "What else is there she'd like me to explain?" he asked. "You're her intended, aren't you,
Mr. . . . er . . . ?" He fished around his pockets for my
note, came up with it already crumpled in a ball and
fumbled with it for the name.

I helped him out and said, "It isn't quite like that.
I'll be completely honest with you, Dr. Foreman.
Mr. Bundy had a namesake in Wisconsin who was
out of touch with him, but who, by accident,
learned of his death. This man apparently believes
there is a family relationship between them and has
asked me to explore the circumstances. There's no
question of a lawsuit, or of any expectations on his
part in the deceased's estate. He merely wants to
know what happened and make sure he's not in any
way concerned. I was informed you were the last
physician in attendance, so I came to you." It was
as close to honesty as I could make it without
sounding like a half-wit from Bohemia, but his ex-

pression as he listened to me was a blend of absent-mindedness and mild bewilderment.

"You'd better see Miss Lord," he said. "As far as I'm aware, she is the only relative he had. Don't know why I confused you with her fiancé. Believe he has a name that starts with *M*, like yours—escapes me what it is. I've got a rotten memory for names."

"Most of us do," I said. "Of course I'll see Miss Lord, as you suggest. There's just one thing, with your permission, doctor. You implied that nothing could have saved the patient, and I'm sure you're right. But I was under the impression that an embolism can be cured these days. One reads about injections, and about an operation for emergencies. . . ."

It didn't seem important, but I meant to draw him out and keep him talking while I had him nailed. He fell for it all right—I'd challenged his professional accomplishments. "Not pulmonary lipoids," he countered testily. "You lawyers are always half informed, it seems to me. You're thinking of a simple blood clot, of the type that may appear in pregnancies or in phlebitis. We've got ways to handle that, with heparin and other decoagulants, or we can operate for it. But Mr. Bundy had an accident last Tuesday night, and broke his leg."

"What sort of accident?"

"He told me he got up to see about a prowler in the yard," said Dr. Foreman with a shrug. "He stumbled on the terrace steps. Miss Lord, who lived with him, managed to reach me right away. I got there in ten minutes, ran him over to St. Mary's in an ambulance. The X ray showed a compound break in the right tibia. We set it, put a cast on it and shipped him home again on Wednesday afternoon."

"And Thursday morning he was dead?"

"That's right, uh-huh. It goes that way. Not often, but it happens. Nothing we can do. Most any fracture, marrow fat may be released and carried up into the body by the veins. It passes through the heart, which pumps it through the pulmonary artery into the lungs. If there's enough of it, it blocks the metabolic function of the tissue, and the patient suffocates."

"After two days?" I asked, surprised.

"Not always, no. Sometimes it takes ten minutes, or a week. Depends on the quantity of marrow fat released and the rapidity of the infusion. It's a risk that anybody takes who cracks a bone."

I pursed my lips, returned his shrug and said, "Sounds fair enough. I take it you were sure."

"Of course I'm sure," he said impatiently. "Think I'd've signed my name on the certificate if there was any doubt at all? I've seen too many pulmonary lipoids, my friend. The symptoms are as clear and unmistakable as anything in medicine. Short breath, a stabbing pain under the ribs, a smothered feeling followed by contortions, death by suffocation, facial cyanosis visibly pronounced. That's all there is to it. I knew the patient well. A healthy man, still in his fifties, who'd been coming in for checkups every year."

"What was his occupation, Dr. Foreman?" I inquired.

He blinked at me. "I'd have to look it up," he said. "Something connected with the picture industry. How does it happen *you* don't know?"

"The only way I ever find out anything is asking questions, just like doctors do," I said, and rose to leave. "I hope Miss Lord will prove as helpful as you've been yourself. What's her relationship to the deceased?''

"His niece," he mentioned absentmindedly. His eyes were on the phone again. "Nice girl. The wholesome type." He actually forced a smile.

"Mind telling me what's her address?" I said.

"She ought to be still living at her uncle's place." He waited, made himself look up, and gestured scoffingly. "I get it. You don't know. Well, ask my office nurse for it, old man, if you don't mind. And if that's all, I wish you would excuse me now." The long, pale, steady hand reached out for mine across the desk and shook it nonchalantly in farewell.

4

DOWNSTAIRS I USED a chromium and plate-glass phone booth in the efficiently chilled pharmacy to call the Arizona Palms in Hollywood. The hotel switchboard offered me a busy signal on the first two tries; third strike brought in a snippy-voiced, gum-chewing operator who said, "Just a minute, plee-uz," and promptly cut me off. My quarter's worth of time had almost run its course when she cut in again. "Whodidchasayyouwant?"

I told her who, again. "Oh, he don't answer. Ifya-wannaleaveamessageI'llconnectchawiththedesk." It ran like pebbles dropped into a can.

The pay-phone circuit operator said, "Your time is up. Twenty-five cents for three more minutes, plee-uz."

I put the phone back on its hook and wandered out into the hard bright yellow morning sun that streamed across the parking lot. The handle of the Pontiac's door was almost hot enough to burn my hand. The dashboard clock announced 10:45. I sat behind the wheel, perspiring quietly, and watched the minute hand creep on another notch or two. I felt as silly as a fireman who's been summoned to put out a cigarette stub smoking in an ash tray. But the day was young, and had been paid for in advance.

The motor started eagerly, as if it loved the exercise. The address was on Mitchell Drive in Crestview Gardens, just a dozen blocks away, a fairly recently developed residential community for citizens of parts. The house was modern Spanish-California and in the $350,000 class, which for that neighborhood was little better than a dump. A waist-high Catalina cherry hedge ran all the way around the formal lawn, patrolled by two large graystone deer. The driveway picket gate was closed. I parked against the hedge and tried the gate, and found it chained and padlocked to its painted iron posts.

Out here this kind of situation doesn't mean much more than that the family in residence desires to keep the Fuller Brush man and the movie fans at bay. I climbed behind the wheel again and crawled around the block. A second driveway lined with jacaranda trees emerged on Essex Road, around the corner, obviously leading straight into the back yard of the Bundy property. The Pontiac's front wheels were already on it when I changed my mind and backed away. There was a light delivery van already parked there, ten or fifteen feet behind the driveway's mouth, and I clicked bumpers with it pulling in along the curb. Its driver slumped into his seat and watched me stolidly while I climbed out and waved at him in casual apology.

The jacarandas thinned around the curve that straightened out into the Bundy motor yard. A row of stately deodars screened off the house, and on my left a copse of early flowering white bridal-wreath spiraea masked the garden court. I'd reached the turf-paved walk that wound around the copse to gain the side porch sheltering the ser-

vice entrance when a burst of fresh young laughter
and the squeal of heavy ringbolts rhythmically grating in their brackets caught my ears.

It wasn't any of my business, of course. But in this
quaint profession most of us develop habit patterns
something like a ham who practices on Shakespeare
every chance he gets. We'll turn our pockets inside
out just to investigate what we've been carrying
around in them. I didn't even stop to think that
time. I ducked into the shrubbery and grabbed myself a load of what was going on. The show was
x-rated but pretty good; you could have booked the
act into the Orpheum downtown for six weeks
straight and turned a lot of customers away. A
properly upholstered garden swing in action always
has been box-office material.

I ducked back out and strolled up to the service
porch behind a grin as big as city hall. My ring
brought forth a very slight and ancient Japanese in
butler's jacket and black pants. The microphone of
an old-fashioned hearing aid was dangling promi-
nently from its shoulder patch; a pair of rheumy
eyes peered at my card through thick-lensed, steel-
rimmed spectacles. The card called me a claims
adjuster for the Mutual Indemnity Assurance Company, which in some cases might be fairly accurate.

He held it off at arm's length, hissed at it, and
bowed to it in rapid, jerky nods—the bows and hisses
definitely for the card and not for me. He gave it
back to me with something of a little flourish.
"Yessah, we insured already. Thank you, preass."

I slipped it back between his wrinkled yellow fingers and said, "Me no sell insurance, savvy? Me ask
questions Missy Lord. From accident to Bundy-
san."

"Oh sso?" This time I got the nods myself. "Okay, preass, you come in." He sounded pretty dubious about it, but a fellow who could speak his language had to be all right. He showed me through a side hall bypassing the kitchen and the dining room, and opening into a sunken living room a trifle smaller than the Philharmonic Auditorium, complete with rosewood Bechstein concert grand, a fine Bokhara rug and six or seven pieces by Matisse or somebody to clutter up the walls.

The living room was nice and cool. Its window blinds were drawn, but light streamed in through the conservatory in the rear. I gave myself a cigarette, admired the Bechstein with its inevitable Paisley shawl, and scrutinized the usual assorted photographs in silver frames it offered on display. There was a formal full-length portrait of a large, bald, floridly complexioned citizen in morning coat and pinstriped trousers, stiffly posed beside a spindly Louis Seize fauteuil. The overall effect was of a cheerful bon vivant who'd run you ragged if you tried to get the best of him in business: the eyes a bit too narrow, nose too sharp, chin prominent and hard as rock. The snapshot next to it, blown up to cabinet size, had him on the beach in swimming trunks, where he looked fit and tanned, if somewhat paunchy, and as proud as Lucifer about the twenty pounds or so of bass hooked on his reel. The next one showed him shaking hands with Darryl Zanuck, both of them in evening dress, and with a plump, attractive blonde in ermine standing by and mugging at him for the camera. He looked a little younger there than in the others—quite a little younger, and a lot less prosperously self-assured. . . .

"Hello!"

They had come in through the conservatory, holding hands. The girl had thrown a terry robe over her shoulders, but the brief white playsuit she'd been almost wearing in the garden was still very much in evidence. It would have looked indecent on some women I could think of, but for her it was just right. She was, as Dr. Foreman had advised, the wholesome type, and could have worn a handkerchief without encouraging the wrong idea. A small brunette, still in her middle twenties, well constructed but by no means beautiful, yet glowing with the kind of charm based on vivacity, contentment and an easy smile. I had to be a nuisance to her, walking in on her like that, but she was smiling for me anyway and greeting me as pleasantly as if I'd been her steady high-school date she hadn't seen in years. I ditched my cigarette and murmured the conventional apologies.

"Yes, I'm Jane Lord. Poor Uncle Jerry never told me he was carrying insurance on himself. Of course it *was* the sort of thing he didn't like to talk about. For him to go like that—you know, I still can't quite *believe* it, honestly I can't. He wasn't really old at all, and just as strong.... Excuse me, Mr. Marshall, this is Bill McHugh. My fiancé."

The boy released her hand, stepped forward and shook mine. He topped my own six feet by anyway three inches, and he had a lot of weight on me, but he was just a lad, not more than twenty-three or -four and pretty as a Christmas package: curly, golden-yellow hair, a sculptured profile and the torso of a football guard. He showed me teeth that would have been an inspiration to an advertising artist with a toothpaste account. Only the grin they illustrated didn't seem to be a match. I had met horses with a brighter personality.

"If I may trouble you, Miss Lord," I said. "A few routine things I'm supposed to ask. I take it you've been left in charge?"

"I guess I have. It's not official yet. Won't you sit down?" She settled on a high-backed love seat by the fireplace, rather gracefully. The boy pitched camp beside her, grabbed her hand again and stared at it as if it were a work of art he'd never seen before. "The lawyers are coming Monday morning with my uncle's will. I know what's in it, though— he told me years ago. He's made provision for the servants, and a rather large bequest to Vera, every-thing considered, but the rest of it...." She shrugged and smiled at me again. "Well, after all, there isn't anybody else."

I dug my notebook out and poised a pencil over it. I didn't need it, but she would expect me to. "Your uncle's name was Jeremiah Peter Bundy?"

"Yes, of course."

"When was he born, and where, please, ma'am?"

"In Rochester, New York, September 20, 1931," she told me promptly. "Don't you know? Surely your company has that on file?"

"They should," I said. "But I'm supposed to ask you just the same. And probably next week they'll mail a form to you that has you go all over it once more. It would annoy me, too, if I were you, but that's what they call claims-verification rules. About his occupation, now—your uncle was a motion-picture studio executive?"

"Well, hardly that." She shook her head and looked surprised with me. "He was a wholesale jeweler. The studios were always borrowing and renting from him, though. You must've heard about the way they operate.''

I wrote it down and said I'd heard, and kept my face in line. It's true enough that Hollywood will never buy a prop, a fur coat or a piece of jewelry. They rent the stuff, and pay a heavy price for it, and still come out ahead somehow. If Frank Brownell was right, they'd probably been jockeyed into renting quite a bit of stolen merchandise.

''He died on Thursday morning, I believe, Miss Lord?''

''A little after eight. I'd just gone up to say good morning and to ask him what he'd like for breakfast when. . . .'' She closed her warm brown eyes and shook her head again. ''It was just *awful*, Mr. Marshall—he was sitting up and feeling cheerful, telling me he'd had a good night's sleep and that his leg had not been bothering him very much. Then suddenly he grabbed himself around the chest as if he had been shot and started struggling for his breath. I ran to phone, of course, and Dr. Foreman was just leaving for his office, so he got here very quickly, but poor Uncle Jerry was already gone!''

I said I understood. The boy McHugh woke up and put an arm around her, scowling at me in a fierce display of what I took to be embarrassment. It was an arm that had more muscle on it than a side of beef; it almost tore the sleeve off his blue polo shirt. Jane Lord moved quietly out of it and blinked the tears away as she glanced up at me in bright inquiry. ''Is that all?''

I said it was except in my report I'd have to mention how he came to break his leg. ''Oh, don't you know? He stumbled on the terrace steps last Tuesday night.''

"How did that happen, please, Miss Lord?"

The boy McHugh said, "Janie, honey..." anxiously as if to warn her off, but she ignored him, fixing me with her determined smile. "I'll always feel it was my fault," she told me frankly. "If I'd had good sense, I should have called the cops and let them handle it. We had a prowler out in back. I heard him when he broke a pane of glass, and like a silly goose I ran to Uncle Jerry's room and woke him up. He seemed excited, even though he never kept a single thing about the house—his stock is always at the bank or in the office safe, and all of it insured, of course. He told me to go back to bed and lock myself into my room, and when I wouldn't he got sharp with me. He had a gun beside him on the night stand, but he had mislaid his flashlight and he said he'd be much better off in darkness, anyway. I tried to talk him out of doing anything, you know."

"He went downstairs? Alone?"

"He wanted me to stay, but I did follow him. Not very close, I'm sorry to confess." She gestured at the double stairway winding up behind me from the front hall. "There wasn't anybody there. They never got inside."

I rose and said, "Mind showing me exactly what your uncle did, and where he fell?"

She was already on her feet. The boy came shuffling after her on his blue denim sneakers, like a big Saint Bernard puppy sniffing at its mistress's heels. We crossed the living room and entered the conservatory with its wicker furniture and terra-cotta floor and hanging baskets of begonias and orchid vines. The French doors to the terrace would have been the customary burglars' picnic if they hadn't been secured by shiny bolts of stainless steel. "Your uncle must have had those put on recently," I said.

"Last week. The old ones weren't much good." She did not seem to think it much of a coincidence. "Here's where they broke the glass."

I squatted down and found some tiny slivers of it still on the conservatory tiles. The pane had been replaced; it was approximately in the location where a man might have reached through and tried to slip the bolts. I didn't think he'd ever got that far along. Most burglars don't make noise, and if they muff a simple job like this, they're usually halfway out to Glendale by the time the customer comes looking for them with a gun. I worked the bolts myself and stepped out on the terrace. "Was it pretty dark that night, Miss Lord?"

She shivered slightly in her robe, regardless of the sun that glared down upon the colorfully patterned crazy paving blocks. "Yes, it was dark, and cold. Poor Uncle Jerry ran right out in it. I heard him shout for me and found him lying at the bottom of the steps."

They led into the garden, six of them, between extensions of the molded concrete balustrade. By daylight there was nothing dangerous about them, but at night it seemed entirely possible to lose your footing there and take a nasty spill. The thing I couldn't figure out was why he'd choose to be a silver-plated idiot and take a chance like that. If he had spotted someone in the shrubbery he could have stayed up there and blazed away at him. No man with any sense would have rushed out into the yard to beg for something like a blackjack on the skull.

"You did eventually get around to calling the police, I hope?"

"As soon as Dr. Foreman and the ambulance had left. They looked around for fingerprints and footprints, the detectives did. They told me they'd be back to talk with Uncle Jerry, but they never came."

"Did he have any visitors at all on Wednesday, after he returned here from the hospital?"

She frowned at me, considering the point. "Just Vera came to see him, Wednesday night. Why do you ask?"

I made myself too busy taking down rough measurements and sketching out the terrace in my notebook to reply. The distance from the sun porch to the steps was forty feet or so; the steps themselves were only six feet wide, perhaps four inches high. "And who might Vera be, Miss Lord?"

"She used to be my aunt. Vera Carstairs, the dress designer at Globe-International. They had been married for a while, but he divorced her years ago. They were still, well, you know, good *friends*."

She sounded mildly disapproving, and the boy McHugh had tacked on his embarrassed scowl again. It would have been a fairly unsophisticated ear that missed the implication, but I let it ride. We drifted back inside, and through the side hall to the service porch; they listened to me say goodbye without pretending more than carefully polite disinterest in my apologies. "You've no relatives in the Middle West, have you, Miss Lord?"

"I may have, on my father's side. I'm not just sure."

"No, ma'am. I'm thinking of the Bundy name. It seems to me I've come across it somewhere—isn't it supposed to be Alsatian in its origin?"

"I'm sorry, I'm afraid I just don't know." The

warm-eyed smile appeared to me a little forced by now. "I thought Alsatians were a breed of dogs?"

This time I took the gravel walk that cut between the deodars into the motor yard. The big four-car garage was closed, but on the tarmac stood a tiny British sports car, gleaming like a June bug in its coat of bright red paint. A handsome pigskin week-end case, two tennis rackets and a large raffia bag crammed full with bathing suits and towels filled the luggage space behind the seats. The dashboard odometer claimed it had been driven all of twenty-seven miles. I pursed my lips at it and marched on down the driveway, climbed aboard my own old bag of bolts and got it under way. The light delivery van that had been parked behind me was still there. I hardly noticed it at all—not until two, three minutes later when it showed up in my mirror while I made the turn from Essex into Wilshire Boulevard.

5

THERE WAS A DRUGSTORE in the middle of the second
block. I pulled up short in front of it and watched
the van swing out into the center lane of traffic,
passing me at a fair clip of speed. It was the quarter-
ton converted Plymouth station-wagon type with
plain dark moss-green panels, often used for parcel-
post deliveries and by department stores. It turned
off Wilshire at the Boscombe intersection, bucking
traffic on the yellow light, and showed a sudden
plume of exhaust smoke before it disappeared from
sight.

I scratched my chin, climbed out and used the
drugstore phone to call the Arizona Palms again.
The Spearmint operator sounded even more preoccupied. From somewhere near her switchboard
came the noise of whistles, catcalls and a barbershop quartet obliging with a slight dissonant rendi-
tion of "Down by the Old Mill Stream." I wrote my
quarter off and used another to call Neil Bodeen,
who bosses the publicity department of Globe-
International. His secretary told me he was in a
meeting, but she'd take a chance and drag him out
for me.

"John boy, where have you been? Long time, no
fun and games."

"How are you, Neil?" I said. "Listen, you're

busy, so I'd better play this straight. Mind fixing it
where I can see your dress designer right away and
have a little chat with her?"

"Carstairs?" His tone was raising eyebrows at me
up to here. "I guess it could be done. What gives?"

"You really want to know?"

"Guess not, if that's the way you put it. Hold the
line—I'll see what I can do." He started muttering
into his second phone, then came back on. "She
isn't on the lot. Her office says they talked to her at
home."

"What's the address?"

He gave it to me between coughs. "Sure this is
nothing we should get steamed up about?"

"You know me, Neil," I said. "I'm always selling
out my friends, but cheap."

"Well, good for you," he heartily approved.
"That's certainly the only way to get along around
these parts. Like me to buzz her and put in a plug?"

I told him not this time, I'd rather handle it
unadvertised, and he invited me to lunch, he was so
eager for a chance to pump me dry. When I refused
we had to waste more time and trade the customary
amiable insults over that. The meeting I had broken
into seemed to have lost interest for him.

Outside I paused a moment in the drugstore doorway, reconnoitering the boulevard. The plain green
van was at the curb, not twenty yards away, three
parking slots behind my car. It had quite simply bar-
reled on around the block. I dug my notebook out
again and jotted down the license number:
2XB0994. The letter serial would indicate a rental
vehicle, the drive-yourself variety. I crossed the
sidewalk, stuck my head in through the off-side
window and surveyed the man behind the wheel.

He wore a peaked black cap without insignia, black whipcord breeches tucked into his boots and a white dress shirt with a black knit tie. He looked more like a private chauffeur than a teamster, if you'd care to hire yourself a chauffeur with a broken nose, black button eyes, no neck to speak of, and a pair of ears like tops'ls in the sunset breeze. Gorilla was too nice a word for him. I grinned at him and mentioned pleasantly, "Watching the watchman, is that right?"

"Don't getcha, Jack," he said. He had a hoarse, uncertain bass, as if he had mislaid a piece of throat somewhere. My sudden turnabout appeared to faze him like the antics of a drunk would faze a bouncer. He was perfectly relaxed, one elbow on the windowsill, the other in his lap, a rancid stub of handrolled cigarette between his thin brown leather lips.

"My point exactly. I don't get it, either. Who're you, and what's the big idea of sitting on my tail?"

"Wrong number, Jack. I never heard of you. I just work here, is all."

"Call that work?" I asked him, pointing with my chin into the empty body of the van. "You bother me, my friend. Get lost before I call a cop."

He did not even blink at me. He merely glanced into his mirror, crooked a hairy finger around the gearshift lever and slid smoothly out into the traffic stream. I scratched my chin some more and stared after the van until it was a dark green matchbox half a mile along the boulevard.

The address Neil Bodeen had given me was on Camino de la Ronda, in the Laurel Canyon hills, and proved to be the dollhouse type of redwood bungalow that realtors insist on advertising as an artist's hideaway. It clung precariously to a sagebrush-

covered granite shelf and came equipped with
honeysuckle trailing from the roof, two stunted
pine trees in the front yard, and a swimming pool.
The pool was big enough to exercise a self-
respecting goldfish in and had been anchored into
bedrock with a cantilevered trestle of concrete that
probably was more expensive than the house.

I left the Pontiac under the house and climbed the
forty flagstone stairs that brought me to the porch.
A handsome black girl in a maid's uniform responded to my knock. She had a little too much makeup
on, but she looked smart enough to be in pictures
for herself. My card did not impress her very much,
although she seemed to know that claims adjusters
haven't anything to sell. "Is Miss Carstairs expecting you?"

"Maybe she is. I can't be sure."

"If she is not, she'll ask me why you wish to see
her, sir."

"It's confidential, I'm afraid. I think she'll understand."

This sort of conversation, stupid as it sounds, is
calculated fairly carefully. It gets you past the servants and the secretaries in this town, but only if
your tone inflection and the face that goes with it
are pitched just right. Even the man who has a
badge pinned in his wallet has to learn this double-
talk and practice it before a mirror if he wants to
make the grade. It is not funny in the least, and I
was slightly startled when the girl quirked up her
lips as if she were amused.

"Will you come in, please, sir?"

The chintzy little living room made do with one
small picture window. It allowed a view across the
canyon of another baker's dozen brush-clad hills.

The harshly incandescent sparkle of the distant ocean glinted through the smog. The maid left me alone in there and closed the door on me. I stood before the window for a while, just looking out, and trying not to sweat so much, and brooding unsuccessfully about the driver of the van. I was unhappy with myself, the way I'd handled him. Somehow it hadn't seemed important at the time—the morning had been wasted on an obviously silly job, and I had let myself get flip with it. The moss-green Plymouth did not fit into the Bundy case. For all I knew it had been tailing me for days, and I had only noticed it on Essex Road because its bumper had got in my way.

That wasn't right, of course. On Wilshire Boulevard the driver had stuck close to me, but down in Crestview Gardens where the traffic had been light he would have kept at least a block between us, if I was his boy. More likely he'd been stationed there to keep an eye on something else, and he had picked me up because I had aroused his curiosity. A certain possibility occurred to me in that respect. I snapped a finger at myself and pounced upon the phone. It waited for me on the polished little Bentwood secretary in the window nook, its ivory-white plastic shell worn dull with use and still retaining a faint wisp of Chanel Number Five.

". . . positively counting on you," said the phone into my ear, before I realized the line was busy. "After all, my dear, it's only money, isn't it?" The voice was masculine, suavely coaxing, coolly self-assured, yet with an undertone of subtly framed intimidation that immediately caught my interest. The dial shield informed me at a glance that this was 555-3468, Extension A. The movie crowd does not go in for party lines.

There was a longish pause, as if the woman needed time to think. Her languid drawl, when it came
on at last, sounded uneasy and harassed. "It's not
the money, sweetie, it's the lack of principle that
worries me. I've tried to tell you that before."

"How terribly discerning of you," said the man.
His breezy chuckle rang with insincerity. "But isn't
it a little late for you to practice self-recrimination,
Vera, dear? If I were you, I should prefer to see the
matter differently, as a simple business transaction,
for example. I feel sure that Jerry would have thoroughly agreed with me."

"He would have knocked that oily smirk of yours
clear through the back side of your head," the
woman told him pleasantly. "But since I haven't
anybody else to do that little chore for me, I guess
I'll have to go along with it. Just bill me, please,
Alfonso, so at least I'll manage to deduct it from my
income tax." The click of disconnection sounded
like a penny cracker going off. I waited for the second click and for the dial tone before restoring the
receiver to its prongs. The hilltops in the picture
window still looked drab with winter brush and
bleary with the smog. Somewhere upstairs the
rapid drumbeat of a pair of bedroom slipper heels
pulsed through the floor.

She swept into the room as if it were a stage, the
chubby blonde who had been in the Darryl Zanuck
nightclub snapshot. She was older now; the fresh
and expert makeup job took off ten years at casual
inspection, but the neckline folds of skin, the
bosom outline and the movement of the hips said
forty-eight or so. The breakfast negligee was
classically styled, of sheer light-orange silk trimmed
with embroidery in silver thread, and zippered to

the throat. The hair was very short and gamin-
esque, and rather obviously tinted to a high and
giddy lemon shade. My card was in one heavily be-
jeweled hand, and being quizzically scrutinized. "If
it's about the costume dress that brazen Walton
hussy burned a hole in with her cigarette, I think
you could have dealt with my assistant at the
studio, young man."

Marietta Walton was the child star they were
building up at Globe that year. I smiled politely,
mentioned I was sorry to intrude at such a time as
this, but that it wasn't anything about a hole
burned in a dress.

"What is it, then? Don't tell me I've got money
coming to me for myself."

I said maybe she did, a lot of it, for all I knew, and
that I was to ask for information on her former husband's death. She stiffened up and glanced back at
my card. "Is that a fact? How very odd."

"Why is it odd, please, Miss Carstairs?"

"Well, I don't know. I can't imagine Jerry buying
life insurance, not as an investment or in any other
way. He didn't need it, and he never seemed to care
for the idea. Besides, you people are a casualty outfit, if I'm not mistaken very much."

"We carry accident insurance," I reminded her.

"I see." She visibly relaxed and settled gracefully
upon a chintzy hassock by the fireplace bay. "What
kind of information? And you might as well sit
down and have a cup of coffee with me and be sociable. Jerry was a louse, but I was pretty fond of
him somehow. I even cried a little at his funeral."

The quilted barrel chair she pointed out was pretty small for me and situated rather closer to her
than convention would prescribe. The maid came in

and brought a silver coffee service while I was still
trying to arrange my legs. She did not speak and left
immediately, but the quirk around her lips remained in evidence.

My wristwatch, when I sneaked a glance at
it, said 12:15. The setup looked as if it had been
fixed for me to earn those hundred dollars after all.
"Just background information, Miss Carstairs," I
said.

Her hands were deftly shuffling cups and coffee-
pot. "You want it black, I guess," she said. "What
kind of background information? Maybe I'm not
very bright this morning, with the head I've got.
You're not suggesting there was something funny
about Jerry's accident?"

"No, ma'am, it's not my job suggesting anything.
You knew him pretty well?"

"He liked that chair you're sitting in. We'd been
divorced for seven years, but he kept dropping up
here when he felt like it. I told you I was fond of
him, which doesn't have to mean that I enjoyed his
way of being married to me. If you're not too young
to understand that sort of thing, my lad."

The coffee tasted fine. It wanted to stand up and
fight, but it had body, zest and enough savor for a
dozen cups. "You never visited him in his house?"

"Sure, I've been there. At Christmas parties and
the like. I've never lived there with him, if you
mean the place on Mitchell Drive. He's only had
that for the past two years. I went to see him there
last Wednesday night after he'd called me from the
hospital."

"He seem all right to you that time?"

"His leg was hurting him, of course. The anes-
thetic had worn off by then." The frown she gave

me was a slightly puzzled one. "He wasn't very talkative."

"Did he discuss the accident with you at all?"

"He told me Jane had heard a prowler early Wednesday morning trying to break in, so he'd got up and packed a gun and run outside to chase him off. He knew it was a foolish thing to do. He wasn't proud of it. Of course he didn't have the faintest notion that the damage was as bad as it turned out to be."

"Miss Lord seemed very nice to me, but not especially affected by it all," I said.

"She never was particularly close to him. Jane's a good kid, perhaps a little prim as girls her age go nowadays. She is his older sister's child—her people have been gone for years and didn't get along with Jerry very well. I think she used to be an airline stewardess until six months ago, when Jerry asked her to keep house for him, because Namura has been getting old and couldn't hold the maids in line. Now I suppose she'll come into his money, and get married to that gorgeous hunk of meat she's been engaged to since they were in high school together, and proceed to raise herself a husky football team."

"He does play football for a living, then?"

"Who, Bill McHugh? Not he—he hasn't got the brains for it. I heard they let him try out with the Rams one time, but he just couldn't get his signals straight. He sells TV sets, door to door. I have one in my den, upstairs, that Jerry bought from him."

I turned my wrist, unostentatiously, to check the time again. I wasn't getting anywhere, and had a luncheon date to keep. "One gathers Mr. Bundy was successful in his business," I said.

Miss Vera Carstairs rose. I hurriedly got up myself, but she brushed by in making for the cellarette behind the little Swedish davenport. "Think you can use a shot?" She did not see me shake my head, not while she bent toward unshipping the decanter, and I was surprised to note she didn't need a girdle after all. "This is a little early in the day for me, but I'm afraid it's either that or aspirin, and I hate aspirin. Last night was sort of rough, if I remember right. Yes, Jerry was successful, in a sense. When I divorced him he'd been barely getting by, but then he must have made some new connections, and of course in my illustrious position at the studio I've managed to throw quite a bit of trade his way."

"Successful in a sense?"

"Oh, Hollywood-successful, if you like. A beach house, and a cottage in the mountains and two Cadillacs, and borrow from the bank to meet a twenty-thousand-dollar Christmas list." She pushed a highball glass into my hand and settled on the davenport with hers. "Sometimes he'd make a flying trip out east and come back with more merchandise than Tiffany's have in their windows, all of it on straight consignment. Maybe he'd sell some of it, but chances were it would turn up on Dorothy Romaine or Betty Leigh in their next musical, and be returned when they were through with it. There's nothing wrong with that, if you can talk the owners into calling it promotion or smart salesmanship."

The highball glass was frosted crystal, duly monogrammed, and tall enough to use for an umbrella stand. It held four fingers' worth of something with a peat-moss flavor, straight. I don't much care for Scotch, but this one spoke up with a burr. The woman watched me sip, and her expression was as thoughtful as a scientist's who is confronted with a rather doubtful specimen of entomology. She touched the cushions of the davenport beside her in a careless gesture of command. "Why make me shout at you this far?"

The distance she complained of was about five feet, but it seemed boorish to debate the point. She leaned away from me once I sat down and crossed her legs to let me see a well-turned ankle, as if we were dallying around with something rather light and charming in a late-Victorian style. I kept my face straight and my nose inside the highball glass.

"Is that a wedding ring?"

I glanced at it as if I'd never noticed it before and said, "It looks like one. It feels like one. I guess it is."

"A pity. Frankly speaking, men have always interested me. More frankly yet, you're probably quite well aware that you're a reasonably handsome lug. Did I say something wrong?"

"Why, no, Miss Carstairs. Not at all."

"I'm going to. It's not the whiskey, either, but I think I've got a right to know. Are you an officer?"

"Not if you mean a cop. They have to introduce themselves as such. They sometimes don't, but only when they're dealing with a crook, or when they can't expect to get information any other way. I have a private license—most adjusters do. In California, that makes a court officer out of you. I'll show it to you, if you want."

"Don't bother, please. I'll take your word for it." For the first time she smiled at me, bewitchingly.

"What made you bring that up?"

"Oh, I don't know. I wouldn't say it was the questions you were asking, not if there's an accident-insurance policy involved. But there's been something in your attitude, my lad. As if you trusted me about as far as you could jump.''

"Which wouldn't be too far right now,'' I mentioned, giving her an amiable leer.

"Don't try to humor me, you beast. I've been around too much for that, and anyway that pretty wife of yours has probably got twenty years and forty pounds on me. Why don't you just relax and tell me of what hideous offense you've been suspecting me? You wouldn't be so childish as to fancy it was me, last Tuesday night, who prowled in Jerry's backyard.... Oh, I get it!'' She was staring past my shoulder at the little Bentwood desk; her sharp, executive-blue eyes were only half amused. "You happened to pick up my phone and caught an earful, sweetie, didn't you?''

I managed to preserve my leer without much effort. "Could be that,'' I said.

"You realize I can make pretty nasty trouble for you, little man?''

"Yes, ma'am, I know you can. Most anybody can make trouble for me if I blow my nose. I wouldn't get much work accomplished worrying.''

She reached behind the davenport for the decanter, and I shifted muscles here and there, in case she meant to brain me with it. "Do they let you handle things for other people?'' she inquired, composedly, as if I were the plumber's journeyman.

It was a situation I'd come up against before. If you take marital-relations cases, which I don't, it's fairly commonplace to have the ''subject'' turn around on you and offer to employ you at a princely fee to put the whammy on your client, a procedure which the license board considers slightly inexpedient. In general investigations this can happen just as well, of course, but there are instances where you can go ahead, because the job you're offered doesn't conflict with the older client's interest, may even be compatible with it.

"Who is Alfonso, Miss Carstairs? What does he have on you?"

"If you must ask, you didn't get it all. Why should I tell you, sweetie, when I can't be sure you'll play the game?"

"No reason why," I said. "Except you can be sure that I won't touch it if you don't come clean, and very possibly not even then. But blackmail is an ugly business. I'm liable to stretch a point, if that's the kind of jam you're in."

Her laugh was almost merry, with its tinkle of polite derision. "Are you thinking of a budget-picture story line? The one about the compromising letters or the one about the woman with a guilty secret? Poor Alfonso, he'd be horrified if he could hear us talk. He runs the *Movieland Observer*, and he only wanted me to buy a little space."

"Oh, *that* Alfonso," I said stolidly.

The *Movieland Observer* was what Hollywood is pleased to call a trade or booster sheet, which signifies a tiny-circulation magazine supposedly devoted to the motion-picture industry. There are at least a dozen, some of them fairly legitimate. Like any other kind of periodical, they all exist on advertising revenue, and space rates come a little high sometimes. A studio that might object to buying six or seven pages just to plug a single major feature for a reader audience of a few thousand of its own competitors is rather likely to be looking at a lot of very bad reviews. Its stars and personalities might suddenly get bushels of the wrong kind of publicity, or none at all.

Mr. Alfonso Baron's weekly journal did not even bother with reviews, the way I'd heard.

"He's tried to put the bite on me before," Miss Vera Carstairs said. "But Jerry took him off my back. He went to see Alfonso, gave him hell, and then invested in a write-up for himself. That was about a year ago. This time, of course, he knows he doesn't have to worry about Jerry anymore. If I get tough with him, he might just possibly pull out the rug from under me."

I understood exactly what she meant by now. I was as sharp as a new pencil in the pocket of an office boy who's bucking for a raise. This was what she'd been leading up to almost from the start. She'd spotted me for something more than an insurance man, and she'd decided to be very frank with me about the color of her associations with the late lamented J.P. Bundy, Esq.

"A top-notch fashion artist wouldn't be too easy to replace," I said. "They've probably known all along about your little weakness, mixing sex and business, up in the front office at Globe. But seeing it in print in the *Observer* might be sort of awkward to explain, back east, to Mr. Moneybags who pulls the strings sometimes when he's upset about our local standards of morality—conflict of interest, and so on. And there's your social life around these parts to be considered, isn't there?"

She sipped her second drink and let her beautifully penciled eyebrows shrug at me.

"How much?"

"I'll see what I can do. I'm not in a position to accept you as a client, Miss Carstairs. Not at this stage.

Next week it may be different, but in the meantime I'll look into it informally, without commitments either way. You probably won't get a bill from the *Observer* until Tuesday, and you shouldn't have much trouble stalling them for a few days.''

"If you can bring it off...." She touched my knee in casual encouragement. "There are a lot of other people in the picture business.''

"Yes, ma'am, I've met a few. You understand I couldn't promise anything, not even if I took the job right now. Sometimes in cases of this type, a character like your Alfonso can be taken care of just by telling him you're putting an investigator on his trail. Sometimes it means a big production, with a crew of us to point a camera at him for months and never shoot a foot of film.''

Her smile was warming up until she caught me looking at my watch again. Then it turned wistful on me, like a little girl's who's being told she can't have more than just one piece of candy.

"Oh, I'm satisfied you'll know exactly how to handle it,'' she mentioned brightly. "Must you go so soon? I've just begun to lose that awful head of mine.''

6

I MADE IT TO THE BEAUTY SHOP by one o'clock.

The little woman tripped across the sidewalk under its marquee the moment I pulled up in front. She wore a sun dress of filmy cotton that clung affectionately to her slim, high-breasted, proudly carried figure, and her elaborately casual auburn curls were fired with copper highlights now. They still fell down to almost shoulder length, I noted with relief. She slid into the seat beside me, slammed the door and kissed me quickly on the mouth.

"You timed that pretty cleverly," she told me. "Angela was late for my appointment, and I was afraid you'd have to wait in there. With all those cats to flex their claws at you. Hey, hey, you've had a drink!"

"That's right. Where do I buy your lunch?"

A truck, disguised with painted cardboard as a railroad engine from the Civil War, went roaring by behind its air-horn blast. It pulled two flatbed trailers, crowded solid with a gang of yelling Bedouins complete with flashing scimitars. The streamer signs tacked on the trailers read Mashid El Akhbar, Tallahassee, Florida.

"Somewhere at least a mile away from all this phony Arab stuff. Did you get through?"

I slipped the car into the garishly kaleidoscopic

traffic on the boulevard and headed west. "Not quite," I wearily confessed.

"Darling, you promised Mr. Bundy a report by noon!"

"He isn't in his room. I couldn't get in touch with him."

"I wondered if he'd started using perfume," Suzy said. She sniffed the shoulder of my jacket in fastidious appraisal. "Very nice. Expensive but discreet. I'd guess Chanel, or Shalimar. Tell mama," she invited me.

"There isn't much to tell, petunia. I interviewed a lot of people, most of them remarkably obliging and informative. I've got the dope the client hired me to dig up, and some to spare. But I'm not happy with the deal. I don't know just exactly why."

"He only wanted you to show him that it was a genuine coincidence, the way he walked into that funeral," she carefully reminded me.

"That's what he said, or rather what he tried to say. Subconsciously he wanted just a little more than that, I think. He felt a funny sort of kinship with the man who died, although it's fairly certain they're not even distantly related. Maybe it was just the heat and the surprise, or maybe he was drunk already, but I've had a queasy sort of feeling ever since I started in on this. And incidentally, it does look as if Frank Brownell was right."

"You mean the second Mr. Bundy was a fence?"

"I mean he was a jeweler. A lot of independent jewelers, at one time or another, are suspected of receiving stolen property. It's more or less an occupational offense, the way malpractice is with doctors or embezzlement with lawyers."

"Well, if he's dead . . . ." the little woman said.

"He is, for sure," I promised her, remembering the mortuary manager who looked like Uncle Ralph.

The car pulled up in front of Eddie's, on the Strip, all by itself. They found a booth for us in there and started feeding us tomato soup, a salmon mayonnaise, iced coffee and black-bottom pie. I took my share of victuals aboard without much real appetite, and answered questions between courses accurately but uneagerly.

"Johnny, that man who followed you sounds very strange. I think you ought to call Dave Hogan and find out about him right away."

"That's what I tried to do when I picked up the phone in Carstairs's living room."

"It's not your job to get into a brawl with characters like that," she chided me. "You're not a cop, and if you were you'd be behind a desk by now, with half a dozen younger men you could send out to do the dirty work. Or at the very least you'd have a partner with you all the time—an extra hand, an extra gun and plenty of authority to use it if the need for it came up. This way you're only asking for a session in the hospital."

"There wasn't any brawl. There isn't any killer, not so far as I can see. Unless you want to figure that this guy was Bundy's prowler, and was therefore indirectly answerable for his death. That's figuring an awful lot too fast."

"I still don't like it," Suzy told me stubbornly. "For a few bucks you're taking chances that a soldier in a foxhole wouldn't have to take." She vigorously stirred the sugar in her coffee glass, as if to emphasize the point. "What is this silly hunch of yours on what our Mr. Bundy really wants, subconsciously or not?"

"Oh, hunch would be too big a word for it. It's probably the heat again, and visiting a cemetery after breakfast—I don't know. Coincidences happen all the time, but this one has an eerie touch. As if there's actually something pretty badly out of joint, and the dead man had to appoint his namesake to clean up the mess."

"He'd have appointed him to go to the police, don't you suppose?"

"Not necessarily. Some people can't afford to deal with them."

"Darling, you must be joking. Surely *our* Mr. Bundy could."

"The fact remains he didn't. But he walked five miles to talk to me. And why'd he get so thoroughly confused at first, pretending he was dead himself and that the funeral had been his own?"

"He was just tight," the little woman said disdainfully. "And if I didn't know you better, Johnny, I'd say you were, too. Although I will admit the other Mr. Bundy's curtain call came sort of sudden, in the middle of the act. Do you imagine there's a possibility his niece or his ex-wife might be involved?"

I blew a perfect smoke ring off my after-luncheon cigarette and watched it drift away. "They both had motive," I said slowly. "But not very much. Miss Carstairs talked as if she didn't even realize she has a legacy from him, but we'll assume she did. She also claimed that his estate would not amount to anything worthwhile, considering appearances. His life was not insured, it seems, and certainly there was no accident insurance, or the company adjusters would already have been on the job. From what I saw and heard, my guess would be he barely

left enough to serve as a temptation for a curve ball
from the heirs. Although both ladies technically
were in a position where they could have thrown
one if they felt inclined.''

"Miss Carstairs saw him on the night before he
died, you told me," Suzy said. "She must have been
alone with him, at least part of the time."

"She claims he called her and asked her to come
down. If they were friends, that would make sense,
and even Jane admits they were. But go ahead and
put the worst construction on it, then what have
you got? She would've had to poison him, is what
you're driving at. What kind of poison would allow
a man to have a good night's sleep, wake up re-
freshed and cheerful, start discussing breakfast,
grab himself around the chest and choke to death
within five minutes? I'm no toxicologist, but I'd feel
fairly safe in offering to take the stuff myself. If
you can tell me where to buy an ounce or two."

"It almost sounds like cyanide," said Suzy
thoughtfully. She pushed her plate and glass aside,
and reached across the table for my deck of smokes.

"Okay," I said. "It sounds like cyanide. It could
have been. That lets out Carstairs, you'll agree,
because the smallest fatal dose will do for you inside of fifteen minutes, half an hour at most. Jane
Lord's still in; she might have slipped it to him in his
medicine on Thursday morning, if he had been taking medicine. Or in a cup of coffee that she
wouldn't mention bringing him, of course. Except
the doctor's going to be there before she can hang
up—he lives three blocks away and she has got to
call him instantly or he is bound to jump on her.
This Foreman chap may be a trifle henpecked and
preoccupied, but he's no fool. He knows the pa-

tient, knows the situation, grabs a sniff of bitter almonds and phones Homicide. Unless you want him to be in on it with her, but in that case he'd hardly take a chance on anything as obvious as that. Even the undertaker might have caught the play."

"Do people go off on a junket to the beach the day after they've buried someone they were living with?"

I shrugged a trifle helplessly and said, "You wouldn't, honey lamb. But you're old-fashioned, which is why I love you dearly. Jane and Bill would seem to be the modern types, less sentimentally inclined. One hears there are a lot of them around. In any case, no matter whom you like or what you may suspect, it isn't any of our business."

"If someone gets away with murder, it is everybody's business," the little woman lectured me unsmilingly.

"I don't agree. We've caught a few ourselves when we were heckled into it, but murder is a job for teams of experts, which we've paid good tax money to hire. If you insist, I'll mention it to Dave and let him play with it. Maybe his boys can figure out why anyone who wants to kill a man would wait for him to break his leg. . . . ."

She frowned and bit her pretty lips for me, and we sat looking at each other rather absentmindedly until the waitress practically pushed the check into my lap. Outside the sun felt like it should be burning holes into the concrete sidewalk. "Johnny, aren't you going to phone?"

"I thought I'd call from home."

"But you're not through down here. You promised Vera Carstairs you would check into that blackmail angle."

"So I did. It almost slipped my so-called mind. Between ourselves, petunia, I doubt if something can be done about it. It's extortion only if you prove the guy is making threats. But if he operates a scandal sheet he's much too slick for that. He doesn't have to threaten, and he doesn't ask for money, period. He's only selling advertising space. If you're not buying, that's all right, and if he prints a pack of lies about you, go ahead and sue. The lies won't hurt you, but the silly, unimportant little facts you can't deny, those are the ones that can be very inconvenient sometimes. They would be for a woman who is prominent in pictures and who likes to put a little business in the way of her 'friends.'"

"You promised, darling," Suzy said.

"I didn't promise, and I don't much feel like working anymore today, but if you really want we'll take a shot at it next week," I said, and pushed into the phone booth of the filling station that adjoined the restaurant.

The voice that said, "Detectives, Hollywood!" was young and flat, and one I'd never heard before. This was a private line into the local sheriff's station, bypassing the switchboard, and I'd used it many times. The voice sounded surprised about a mere civilian using it. "Not in," it said succinctly. "What's the name again?"

I gave the name again. "Does the lieutenant know you, Mr. Marshall?"

"When he wants to. Is he out to lunch?"

"No, sir, he's gone off duty. Any message, please?" I said there was no message and hung up. The phone book, dangling from its rusty chain below the pay-phone slot, supplied the *Movieland Observer*'s number and its office address in the Sub-

way Circuit Building within spitball range from the
old Arizona Palms. I scowled at it and shook my
head, dug up another quarter and invested it in one
more dubious connection with that worthy hos-
telry. "His room don't answer. Ifyawannaleavea-
message...."

"Yes. I do."

The Spearmint operator almost swallowed it from
sheer surprise, and slammed the jack into a plug.
Someone said "Murphy, desk!" against a background noise of beating drums and rebel yells.
"Bundy? Six-twenty-nine. He's out."

"You're sure of that?"

"Key's in the rack. Excuse me, please." He
clapped his hand on the receiver, but not hard
enough; I caught the rumblings of a fairly heated
argument off-mike. "... can't bring a horse into the
lobby, sir. Manager's orders. Murphy, desk! Yes, sir,
one moment, please. Hello! Who did you say you
wanted?"

"J.P. Bundy, in six-twenty-nine. Just put a note
in with his key that says John Marshall called,
and...."

"Six-two-nine, John Marshall, right." The line
clicked dead. I grunted and hung up. The little
woman watched me coming out and smiled at me in
sympathy. "You'd better use a hanky, darling."

"Little close in there," I said, and followed her
advice. "Dave took the afternoon. He must be sick,
or crime is on an unexpected holiday. The client's
still A.W.O.L. What time did you leave home?"

"A quarter past eleven. Alice Holt next door gave
me a lift."

"I couldn't reach him at a quarter to, this morning, so it looks like he went out without attempting

to call me. But things are in a mess downtown. Maybe we'd better run on in and hunt him up."

"He's probably off on another binge and has forgotten all about it," Suzy said after I'd turned the car around and we were rolling east again. "Darling, can we afford to buy a freezer?"

"Huh?"

"Alice was telling me about the one she got from Joe for Christmas. How she's buying all her meat and frozen vegetables wholesale, and she never has to bother shopping anymore. Imagine steaks at ninety cents a pound, as many as you want, and stored right on your service porch!"

"It sounds expensive, sugar plum."

"I know. The box is something like three-fifty, plus a lot of taxes, and this wholesale thing is only talk. I pinned her down, and what she has to do is buy a half of beef. They cut it up for her, of course, but most of it is chuck or ground, and it's not really ninety cents, it's ninety-eight. And on the vegetables all she saves is three-four pennies on a package, if she buys them by the dozen, which is less than I can save by watching for the specials at the store."

"Four hundred skins is money," I reminded her. "The house needs painting, and the carpet in the living room has spots you can see through. If we were farmers, living off our own produce . . . .".

"Sometimes I wish we were," she wistfully confessed. "Sometimes it seems to me as if they are the only people in the world who have a really worthwhile job and who don't have to take in other people's washing. . . . Johnny, there he goes!"

"Who, Mr. Bundy?"

"No, dear, it was Dave. He turned the corner over there while you were fiddling with the radio."

"*That* horny-handed son of toil," I said, and skidded in a screaming U-turn through the nearest traffic gap. The intersection she had pointed out led into Juanita Canyon and across into the San Fernando Valley, where Lieutenant David Hogan owned a tiny chicken ranch. His weathered, elderly black Ford sedan was half a mile inside the canyon, chugging steadily uphill, when we caught sight of it. I stuck my foot into the carburetor, leaned an elbow on the horn and sizzled by to cut him to the curb.

He waited for us, slumping down behind the wheel, a stocky little Irishman in fairly well-preserved late middle age, white haired and shaggy browed, gray leather-faced, his clear blue baby eyes blankly expressionless. The open collar of his vividly Hawaiian sport shirt was as clean and stiffly pressed as if he had just put it on; he knew he couldn't book the sun on charges of assault and battery. I dragged my notebook out, produced a pencil, scowled at him forbiddingly and said, "You in a hurry, mister? There's a judge downtown that don't like people in a hurry. Lemme see the driver's license, please."

He might have grinned, if he'd remembered how. Some of them do, sometimes, but he'd seen thirty years of service, mostly on the sheriff's Confidential Squad, which meant he was a cop who often had to put the screws on other cops.

"I should of known," he sourly complained. "Day captain borrows half my boys on slush detail for the parade. The boss himself has got a bed sheet on so he can ride in it. My brooder's conking out with sixty Leghorn chicks, and now I got this half-assed private schnook in sharkskin pants that wants to clown me up. Okay, already, Johnny, what's the beef?"

"Oh, Dave!" the little woman said commiseratingly. "How wonderful you are, the way you're bearing with it all. We'll try to make it up to you somehow."

"Of course he's only got himself to blame," I said. "You notice that with half his fly bulls rousting dips and grifters off the streets he can still spare one to play tag with me."

"He wouldn't," Suzy told me earnestly. "He's sweet, and kindly, and considerate. He'd call you first and ask you nicely for the information if he thought you might be holding out on him. He'd never do a sneaky, despicable thing like having someone follow you around to see what you were up to. Would you, Dave?"

"Could be," said Hogan, turning off his engine pointedly, as if reminding us about the waste of county gasoline.

"I think you're right," I said. "This character I dusted off my tail had bat ears and a broken nose. He was too pretty for a cop in Hollywood."

The shaggy brows went up for me a fraction of an inch; the clear blue baby eyes looked through me at the distant scenery. "Where was you at when he was tailing you?"

"Beverly Hills, this morning. So he *was* a cop," I said.

"What're you working on?"

I pursed my lips at him. The little woman said, "Why, Dave, we're flattered you should ask. But if you know already, what's the use?"

He casually glanced at her and turned the key in his ignition lock back on. A motorcycle deputy in

summer khaki snarled around the canyon bend, cut
throttle when he saw us, recognized the Ford and
coasted by downhill, elaborately unconcerned.

"You kids got time, we'll go back to my office,"
Hogan said.

"What for?"

"I wanna show you something, is what for."

We kids looked at each other, shrugged in resignation. "Lead the way, Lestrade," I said.

"Who's he?"

"He was a cop. In London, England, way back
ninety years ago."

"I never heard of him. Let's shake the lead."

He shook it hard enough to get us back to town in
fifteen minutes flat. It was good time without a
siren, plowing through the crowds already gathered, waiting for the big parade to start. He waved
us on into the empty prowl-car parking lot at twenty after two, according to my dashboard clock, and
strode ahead of us into the coarsely whitewashed
stucco box that was the station house. The dingy
imitation marble stairs rang hollowly under our
feet. The building seemed too quiet, almost
deserted—on the second floor a row of doors stood
wide ajar. Hogan stood waiting for us patiently to
hold the one that bore no painted legend other than
a fading number 25. Behind it were four walls, a
hardwood floor, a battered civil-service desk, three
straight-backed chairs, an ancient water cooler and
a filing cabinet. The cleaning woman's mop and
Lysol hadn't quite been able to remove the stale
cigar smoke and the reek of every crook since Judas
in that room.

"This him?"

It was a reader flimsy, riffled out from scores of

others on a pin, and folded back to let me look at just the mug in front and profile views. The blackboard sign between them said PD ST LOUIS MO 248241. I took it over to the window and studied it while Suzy peeked over my elbow. "Nice," she said admiringly. "A schoolgirl's dream. Who is he, Dave?"

Hogan sat down behind the desk, ignoring her and watching me. I threw the folded reader on his blotter, shrugged and gave myself a cigarette. "What do you want him for?"

"We wanna talk to him, is all. Why was he tailing you?"

"I've no idea."

"That right? What're you working on?"

"Let's understand each other, Dave," I said. "We phoned you after lunch to tell you about that, but you'd already left. We caught you on the road for the same purpose, not for you to drag us into this and throw your weight around. We haven't any ax to grind or information to suppress. You're welcome to the story, inconclusive as it is. But not this way, and not until we know the reason why."

He stared deadpan across the room at the big wall map of the County of Los Angeles—four thousand square miles of lush beaches, snow-capped mountains, orange groves and city blocks, and sin. "You make the guy?"

"I make his mug. That's all I know, so far."

"Bat Wiley is the moniker that goes with it. Second banana in Max Ulrich's mob. That mean anything to you?"

I shook my head. He jabbed the buzzer on his inter-office phone. A heavyset young man in beautifully tailored flannel slacks, brown rayon sport shirt, and a face as vacant as the brand-new holster strapped into his belt, walked in through the communicating door and looked us over without interest. "Pull Maxie Ulrich's package," Hogan told him carelessly.

"Yes, sir. You want the Central Records file, Lieutenant?"

"You kidding? Should I wait an hour for you to travel to the Hall of Justice and come back? They got a subfile down at Homicide."

The man in the brown sport shirt clicked his heels and smartly marched offstage. Hogan glanced after him, sardonically disapproving. "College boy. Three months in traffic school, six months on crosswalk duty. Now he's a detective on my squad. You got to draw a map for him so he can find the john."

"This Ulrich is a killer?"

"Yeah, he's pretty hot. The Feds are kind of sore at him about a mail-truck heist in Springfield, Illinois, five hundred grand in unset diamonds. They caught the finger on that job. He squealed, but Maxie blew to Mexico. They took him last October, down to Vera Cruz or some damn place, after he'd fogged a couple of 'em in a shooting match. They sent him up for life."

"They didn't get the bundle?"

"Post-office inspectors say they didn't. Me, I wouldn't know. They talked to Maxie in the calaboose down there the day before his sentence. He just laughed at 'em."

Suzy turned from the window with a puzzled frown. "This man Bat Wiley that you want us to identify," she said. "Is he supposed to have the diamonds, Dave?"

"Could be. We got no evidence he was involved.

The finger don't know anything about him, but Saint Loo claims him and Maxie was mobbed up for years."

"There must be more to it than that," I said. "Or else you wouldn't even have the file on tap."

"You wanna make a buck?"

"How's that again?"

"You heard."

"I couldn't have. It sounded like you asked me did I want to make a buck."

"So what's to be surprised, already? You're in business. You got a license, you put up a bond. The law says we're supposed to leave you make like an investigator, don't it? Listen, Johnny, there's ten grand reward in this for you."

"Is that a fact," I said. "Who's putting up?"

"The underwriters. Lloyd's."

"Why, Dave, you *are* a doll," the little woman said. She made it sound as if this were a garden party and he'd offered us a cup of tea.

"Ten thousand dollars isn't such a lot of dollars," I reminded him. "Not for a job that's liable to take six months, on spec, in competition with their own organization and the Feds. What's coming off here, anyway? What makes *you* care?"

The dick in the brown sport shirt marched back in and laid a thin red cardboard file on Hogan's desk. He left without another glance at us; he was the most incurious cop I'd ever come across. Hogan leafed casually through the file and tossed another circular into my lap. This time he did not bother folding it. It was a post-office department mug sheet, four months old, and advertised one Maximilian Norman Ulrich, also known as Max the Dude, said to be Wanted for the Crime of Robbing Mails of

the United States. The front and profile art was
tabbed PD ST LOUIS MO 248240, and showed a face
so commonly arranged as to be almost nondescript:
round, smooth, expressionless, with not a single
feature disproportionate. The shoulders bore a
neatly pressed gray herringbone, the stodgy Middle
Western dress-shirt collar hid behind a flashy
polka- dot bow tie. There was a sprawling sample
signature and a description: *Born Milwaukee;
white; age 30; height, 5'8"; weight 157 lbs; eyes
brown; hair black; complexion medium; build
medium; well- dressed in business attire. This man
is armed and dangerous. He frequents race tracks,
theaters and nightclubs, is extremely fond of female
company and is a lavish spender. Arrest on sight
and notify the undersigned at once by telephone or
teletypewriter, collect. See other side for fingerprints.* The fellow who insisted upon paying for
your phone call was one C.A. Egglesmithers, Post
Office Inspector, Springfield, Illinois.

"That's nice," I said, and gave it back to him.
"You're nice. The world is nice. Where do we go
from here? This piece is slightly out of date."

"You think so? Maxie busted jail a couple weeks
ago."

"Maybe he didn't like tortillas," I said slowly,
watching Hogan narrowly. I'd caught the pitch by
then, not very fast, and meant to swing at it about
as hard as if it were a stick of dynamite.

He pushed across a yellow scratch-pad memo,
holding on with two broad horny finger tips that
covered nothing of the scribbling on it but a single
word in the top line: *Lt. Hogan:. . . . . .phoned and
says that Max the Dude's in town. No make on his
10-20, but he's gunning for Kicks Henderson who*

crossed him on the Springfield caper. Do we talk to Kicks, or do we pull a stakeout on his joint? 1/17, 9:25 a.m., O'Reilly, Homicide. Below, in neatly printed little caps, a second pen took over: *Leave it lay for now. D.H.*

The seventeenth was Saturday. Today. I grinned and said, "Your stoolie missed the bus."

The clear blue baby eyes were cynically unconcerned. "Maybe you know a better snitch. Listen, I passed the ball to the P.O. They're flying in a team from San Antonio that's been assigned to Maxie all this time. They'll push him over in the end, but that don't mean I'm satisfied. We got like fifty thousand ex-cons in this county, on account they like the climate is the way I hear. You figure I can use a couple of them heist guys from Missouri on my reservation that I got to hold still for and let the Feds take off my hands, because my men are working this convention of a bunch of jerks in bed sheets that has named the boss a Grand Vizier or some damned thing?"

I glanced at Suzy, saw her face and shook my head decisively. "No sale," I said.

The shaggy brows went up and down. "Who's peddling? I just figured maybe you could use the dough. What're you working on today?"

I told him what, in Technicolor and in consummate detail. He listened patiently enough, the silent, weary patience of a seasoned operator with the fumblings of a semipro. It lasted ten or fifteen minutes, and toward the end his craggy leather face had set itself into a mask of boredom and indifference. "This guy that hired you was a lush?"

"Well, what about it? I've explained to you the reason why I had to take him on. That doesn't have a thing to do with it."

"Could be."

"Why, David Hogan, I'm surprised with you," the little woman said indignantly. "We came to you like people, to report a death under suspicious circumstances, and the only thanks we get are snide remarks about the clients we accept. If that's the way you feel, let's just forget it and pretend we never bothered you with this at all."

The grooves around his grimly weathered mouth twitched briefly in amusement. "Sure now, what's the fuss? I didn't knock you kids. You got to make a living, same as everybody else."

"You realize there may be a connection with this Ulrich case," I said. "If so, that broken leg was certainly no accident. The niece's testimony isn't worth a dime on that account. She says herself she didn't really see what happened on the terrace steps."

"That ain't for you to kick around."

"Suits me," I said. "I'm happy if you are. You boys get paid a handsome salary for coping with this sort of deal."

"Can't beat police routine," he smugly promised me. "Nobody can."

The little woman hooked an arm through mine and steered me firmly out into the corridor and down the phony marble stairs. We were already blocks away and pushing slowly through the crowds when it occurred to me he hadn't even asked me for the license number of Bat Wiley's rental van.

7

THE BIG PARADE HAD STARTED, so we had to circle all
the way around by Western Avenue to find an open
intersection that would let us cross the boulevard. I
drove back into town on Franklin, which was rela-
tively quiet, and turned into the side street that ran
down into the main drag past the Arizona Palms
Hotel. There were no legal parking spaces left in
Hollywood, but they will let you park before a fireplug if there's someone at the wheel. I found one in
the middle of the block and set the hand brake, left
the motor running and smiled for the little woman
in benevolent dismissal. "This is close enough for
you, bright eyes."

"What do you mean?"

"I mean you take the heap and go on home. I'll
grab a cab after I'm through."

"Why can't I go with you?"

The brass band marching by a hundred yards
away was pounding out "Hail to the Chief." The
crowds broke into cheering and applause. "Because
I want you to go home!" I shouted over it.

"John Marshall, you're not just about to take a
shot at that reward!" she stormed at me.

I grinned and shook my head decisively. She had a
handful of my shirt and firmly pushed me back
against the seat. "You can't go up against those

hoodlums by yourself! I won't allow it, do you hear?''

"To hell with the reward!'' I yelled.

She nodded in approval and released my shirt. "Then if you're only looking for the client, I can save you cab fare if I stay right here."

"But it may take a couple of hours. And you might have to move the car!''

She turned the engine off and set her stubborn little chin. I shrugged and kissed the tip of it, and hit the street. The brass band had moved on, and in its place a string of gaily caparisoned circus elephants were ponderously waddling by. The rear ranks of the crowd were only twenty yards away and blocked the shopping arcade and the bar of the hotel. I started infiltrating tactics and had almost made it when some jolly soul up on the sidewalk next to the parade route tossed a cannon cracker at the nearest elephant.

It burst with a convincing thunderclap. The startled animal backed off, slipped on the streetcar tracks and lurched into the sidelines with its trunk aloft and trumpeting distress. There was a sudden roar of panic all around. The crowd surged in on me and swept me clear across the street. A drugstore window shattered and a woman in a torn blue dress lay in the gutter, moaning, with her face a ghastly smear of blood and dust. I dug my heels into the pavement, charged in her direction, made three yards and met another surge that carried me around the drugstore corner to the boulevard. Its backwash put me with a score of red-faced, sweating, jostling people in the lobby of an office building, six doors down the block. Outside, the circus mahout had already managed to regain control. The elephant was lumbering along; another military band came marching in its wake behind the cartwheel antics of a dozen majorettes in bathing suits and gold-cockaded busby hats.

I used a handkerchief, removed my coat and looked around. The building's tenants' index almost hit me in the eye. It listed chiropractors, music publishers, mail-order agencies, a credit dentist, and the Movieland Observer Company, Incorporated, Suite 512.

I winced and gave the board a careful and uneasy double-take. Most all of us have been occasionally nudged by destiny, but what I felt came closer to a kick, and from a cloven hoof.

My watch said three o'clock. I glanced at it mechanically, entering the elevator, hardly pausing to consider that a weekend afternoon in Hollywood is for the janitor to put his feet up on the boss's desk. The corridor on five was cool and dark, and not particularly clean; the noise of the parade sounded a mile away. The pebbled-glass door marked 512 displayed a fancy monogram "MO" in letters three feet high. I put a pair of shell-rimmed dark green glasses on, took off my tie and ran a hand of fingers through my hair. The door swung open readily. I would have fainted it if had been locked.

The small reception room was done severely functional in scarlet leather, black frieze and stainless steel. There were two desks, both unattended, shoved together in the window bay; the typewriter on one of them was hooded, but the big electric I.B.M. comptometer invited me to flip a switch and figure up the week's receipts. The only picture on the redwood-paneled walls was of a poker-faced

Saint George in eighteenth-century-style copper-
plate, the dragon gory but defiant as the broad-
sword plunged into its heart. A second door cut
through the panelwork beyond the picture and proclaimed in chastely modest goldleaf printing Office
of the Publisher.

I knocked and walked on in; and there he was, of
course, as specified.

His Chinese lacquered working table had been
raised a foot or so up on a glass brick dais to
separate him from the common herd, which had to
be content with an Armenian rug and three white
quilted-vinyl armchairs grouped around a smoking
stand of hammered bronze. Two walls were lined
with books, immaculately bound and dressed like
soldiers, most of them expensive presentation sets.
The third was covered with at least a hundred
glamour stills of motion-picture personalities, most
of them female and galvanically autographed.

Mr. Alfonso Baron sat behind the table on the
dais. The teakwood carving on his high-backed
judge's throne came to its apex in a Roman wreath
above the artfully styled crown of his corn-blond
scalp. He seemed to be engaged in plowing through
a stock of illustrated movie magazines, the kind
that caters to the fans, like *Photoplay*, *People* and
Modern Screen.

"What do you want?"

He'd sized me up in one quick, startled glance and
had immediately decided he could buy me at the
five-and-dime. He was no bargain-counter specimen himself, by any means, I had to give him that.
His face and body matched his carefully groomed
hair and the custom-tailored, Pierre Cardin blazer,
the St. Laurent shirt.

I let my voice come up a full octave and put a jitter into it. "The name is Marshall, Mr. Baron, and you've never heard of me, I'm sure. But I've been reading the *Observer*, and I think it's only great. I mean the job you try to do for Hollywood."

He fell for it; they always do. There are no members of the population being built impervious to flattery, but in this town they are so hungry for it you can feed them plain baloney, duly labeled and identified as such, and they'll sit up and beg for more. He didn't think my contribution rated me important, but I had his ear. "You're in the business?"

"The picture business," I said. "Ah, yes. I'm in it, up to here. I am indeed."

That brought a thin but understanding smile, the lordly type. "Don't like it much, do you?"

"A dirty mess," I said, and delicately touched a finger to my nose. "But positively *rank*, you know. It's just exactly like you're always pointing out in the *Observer*, Mr. Baron. What we ought to have is someone to clean house and give us back our self-respect. From where I sit, I've seen some of the most disgraceful things since Genghis Khan, you know."

"Have you? Where do you sit, my friend?"

"I'd be ashamed to tell. I really would."

His lip curled up a little more. "Perhaps there's something I can do for you."

"For all of us," I said, and took my glasses off to look him in the eye, as manly and sincere and fatuous as I could make it. "You're already doing that. You are indeed. I'd like to help."

He let the smile fade out. So far he hadn't even offered me a chair. "I'm always welcoming suggestions from our readers," he said distantly.

The brassy strains of "Dixie" filtered up to us through the closed windows from the boulevard.

"Suggestions," I said earnestly. "You wouldn't need suggestions, Mr. Baron, not from me. Or anybody else. I know that much."

"What do you think I need, my friend?"

I would have loved to tell him, but instead I said, "Ah, well. Perhaps I'm wrong. One tries. So sorry and all that."

He let me drift until I touched the doorknob. "Just a minute, Marshall. What precisely did you have in mind?"

"It happened to occur to me you might be interested, Mr. Baron. In these charming people I run errands for. The hanky-panky and the goings-on, you know. The stuff they get away with and nobody slaps them on the wrist." I slapped my own to show him how, not very hard.

The lofty smile was back on tap. "Sit down," he ordered me. "Which studio?"

That signified the hook was going in. He didn't trust me yet, but he was willing to be shown. I wasn't happy with him either; roping crooks is quite an art, which normally requires a lot of preparation, patience and a carefully established front. I'd let myself be pushed into a quickie job against my better judgment, and the chances were I couldn't make it stick. The average extortioner is not an easy fish to catch. Proper technique involves investigating him until you hit on something that will handle him if he gets out of line. This will come off in many cases, but it usually takes a lot of time. I was already scouting for a handy spot in which to plant a bug, next week.

"I work for Globe," I said. "Publicity. If you can

bring yourself to dignify it by that worthy name. When Neil Bodeen wants to send out for hooch, or for a stick of tea, he rings for me."

The tall blond man with the suavely vicious face sat very still and studied me as if I had just introduced myself in the capacity of his intended future son-in-law. "I see," he said at last. "An interesting matter of coincidence."

He took his eyes off me and let them roam about. They rested briefly on the squat green safe that sat behind me in a corner, swept the wall with its array of fervent autographs, and landed on the phone, behind the stack of magazines, within his reach. He reached for it and picked up the receiver, put it back again. I had a bit of difficulty hanging on to my expression of lavender innocence. There was no reason to believe that Neil Bodeen would even speak to him.

"The hanky-panky and the goings-on," he said, almost reflectively. "You put that rather well, my friend. I wonder if you realize how much of it there is." He riffled through his stack of magazines and jerked one out and threw it at me, half across the room. It landed on the smoke stand with a bang. "Page thirty-two," he barked at me.

I flinched for him like he'd expect me to, and looked. Page thirty-two was a full-color still of Dorothy Romaine, a Globe star from way back, in show-girl costume, war paint and a peacock feather fan. The caption mentioned *Vegas Cavalcade*, a fifties period-piece musical released about a year ago. The magazine was a back copy from the morgue. "Ah, yes," I said. "Of course. But certainly. Our little Miss Walpurgis Night of 1968. Want me to see what I can conjure up on *her* for you?"

He shook his head impatiently. "Not now. Describe the jewelry she's wearing there."

I had suspected that was it. Now that we'd got that far along, I had to figure out what I could do with it. "Large ruby diadem," I said. "Pearl choker, six or seven strands. Four diamond bracelets, two of them combined with square-cut emeralds. Two diamond-and-ruby rings. Why are you interested, Mr. Baron? None of those belong to her, you know. We rent the stuff from someone in the trade."

"I'm well aware of that," he said. His eyes were drilling me again. He was in trouble, struggling with himself about how far I could be trusted, if at all. He finally came to the only logical decision, from his point of view. "Who'd be responsible for renting jewels in your shop?"

"Carstairs," I told him instantly. "The needlewomen's tyrant queen."

He nodded solemnly, as if allowing me an A for effort. He dug up another sheet and marked it with a pencil ring, and pitched it in my lap, less churlishly this time. It was a copy of his own *Observer*, dated a few weeks before the picture magazine. The front page bannerhead screeched in fat upper case H'WOOD MUST WIPE OUT DOPE, SEX MANIACS, SEE EDITORIAL ON PAGE THREE.

The pencil ring was on page two, and drew attention to an item somewhere halfway down the featured gossip column, "Keyhole Peeks." It coyly asked, *What ritzy BevHills jeweler may have to change his morning coat for something with a number on the back?*

I made a show of puzzling over that before I let myself pretend to see the light. "Oh, grand," I said.

"But positively elegant, you know. You're sure of this, of course?"

"If I'd been sure, do you suppose I would have dropped the matter there?" he scoffed at me. He watched my face fall into lines of disappointment and afforded me his thinly chiseled smile. "I'll be completely frank with you, my friend. The only thing I knew to be a fact when this was written, was that Miss Carstairs had once been married to the man, that she had continued to maintain an intimate relationship with him, and to use her position at the studio to help him in his business."

"You were just guessing at the rest of it?"

"An educated guess, or so it proved to be. He came to see me at the time and managed to convince me that I was misjudging him. But information reached me yesterday to the effect that he was definitely known to the underworld as a receiver of hot jewelry."

"He *was*?"

"He had an accident this week and died two days ago."

I let him see me think it over, hard. By then I had a fairly good idea what he was driving at. A crook remains susceptible to crooked propositions, even those that do not fit his speciality at all, and that he is as competent to handle as a carpenter is competent to bake a wedding cake. His problem now, so far as he could tell, was to enlist what help I might be able to supply without arousing my suspicion of his purposes. My problem was to take advantage of the deal to where he'd paint himself into a corner in some way.

"Ah, well," I said regretfully. "A man can die but

once and all that sort of thing. Of course there's still the charming Miss Carstairs to reckon with."

Mr. Alfonso Baron fixed me with a sternly speculative eye. "The question is, my friend, whether she was his dupe or his accomplice," he reminded me.

DOWNSTAIRS, THE CROWDS of rubbernecks were breaking up and going home. The tail of the parade was clearing Highland Avenue, some fifteen blocks along the boulevard. Two clerks were boarding up the corner drugstore window, and the woman in the gutter had been carted off by ambulance. I put my coat and tie back on and used a pocket comb, and navigated with the current down the side street and across.

The Arizona Palms was fairly easily accessible once more. I reached its porte cochere and paused to glance back down the street toward the Pontiac. It was still parked beside the fireplug, and the brittle January sun reflected harshly from its windshield, eighty yards or so away. I frowned at it, for no good reason I could think of, and administered a dose of shoulder to the sluggishly revolving doors of the hotel.

Inside the big dark lobby was a noisy mess, filled with the crashing surf beat of tumultuous hullabaloo made by the customers. Some six or seven hundred turbans and burnooses in all the colors of the rainbow milled about the place. Green, white and crimson streamers draped the Gothic colonnades of the grand ballroom stairs where Theda Bara used to make an entrance in the days of silent films, and where the Keystone Kops would practice sliding down the banisters. The lobby's normal

decoration scheme of half a dozen wilted giant
aspidistras had been slightly modified with cardboard jungle vegetation, half a ton of desert sand, a
Moorish fountain and a tabernacle tent that featured snake charmers and harem girls.

I waded through to the reception desk. Four shirt-
sleeved clerks in purple turbans were behind it,
struggling with the tide. The key-rack pigeonhole
marked 629 was in plain view. It held a large brass
key with an old-fashioned composition tag, and
showed the edge of a pink message slip.

"Yessir?"

"Calling on Mr. Bundy," I said diffidently, pointing at the rack. "I've tried to get ahold of him all
day. Don't seem to have much luck with it."

The clerk bestowed a weary smile of sympathy on
me and speared the message slip between two fingers, checking it. "You're Mr. Marshall, sir?"

"That's right."

"One moment, please."

He ducked into the office of the manager, behind
the rack. I didn't see how that would help, but I was
glad to let him work it out. He took a minute and
came back without the message and without the
smile. "I'm sorry, sir. We seem to have no information for you here."

"That's an odd way of putting it," I said, and
leaned an elbow on the hairy flank of the stuffed
camel parked beside the desk. "You're sure he isn't
in his room?"

"Quite sure," the clerk insisted solemnly.

"Know him by sight? Seen him at all today?"

"No, sir, I haven't. Have you tried the cocktail
lounge?"

The camel had a funny odor, and its yellow hide

was warm. It stirred a little, turned its head and looked me in the eye, maliciously. I hurriedly removed my elbow, spoke a naughty word and plowed into the surf again.

The cocktail lounge seemed like a sensible suggestion anyway. Its lobby entrance was behind the harem girls; its front was on the side street where my car was waiting, next to the arcade. It was the Mexican cantina type, with ornamental iron furniture, a polished red-tiled floor and bullfight posters on the mock adobe walls. They had more clientele in there than they could hope to serve by Labor Day, but they were holding up their end. The joint was jumping clear across the moon.

I'd made a start at giving it a frisking when I saw the little woman enter through the side-street door and set a course toward the bar.

A small supply of ice cubes in my stomach promptly made its presence felt. She'd risked a high-priced parking ticket, and she'd risked missing connections with me. That wasn't like her at all. I plunged into the mob to intercept her, made six yards for a first down and watched a sheeted, turbaned gentleman from Arkansas or Maine go stalking her with an electric cane. The buzzer point was reaching for her skirt hem when she spun around and kicked him smartly in the shins. I bulldozed in between them while he was still hopping on one foot, and blocked him off.

"What happened, angel face?"

"Oh, Johnny, where've you *been*?" Her hand clutching my arm was shaking, and she'd lost a lot of healthy color from her pretty tan. "He was in here, but they came after him! They've taken him away!"

"Who's they?"

"Darling, I just don't know. There were two men, and they were dragging Mr. Bundy out with them into their car. I saw them doing it, and still I couldn't even tell you what they're like."

"You recognized him?" I demanded carefully.

She nodded eagerly while I was herding her into a corner by the service door. "Of course I did. He struggled with them and I ran to help him, but they were too quick for me. I've been just *frantic* for you to come back!"

"How long ago was this?"

"Maybe ten minutes—the parade had just gone by. The car drove up a little earlier, and turned around. They left it double-parked in front of the arcade."

I stared at her. It wasn't hard to get the picture, though I couldn't make much sense of it. I'd parked the Pontiac with its nose toward the boulevard. The other car had passed it, made a U-turn and so put itself in a position for an easy getaway. "Where you slipped up, petunia," I said, "was when you got out from behind the wheel and tried to tackle them on foot. You would've had a chance to nail them if you'd pulled our bag of bolts across the street. But maybe it was just as well you didn't think of it. You catch the plates?"

It was a Texas license, 4A413, a rust-brown Chevrolet sedan; she'd made a lipstick note on Kleenex, folded twice. That made it sound still worse. I didn't understand it, but it seemed a cinch I wouldn't like it if I ever did.

"Why'd you decide to come in here instead of waiting for me, cherry pie?"

"You took so long. I couldn't take it, sitting there

and marking time. I thought I might pick up some information in this place."

"It's possible," I said, and glanced around. A dozen waiters and three barmen were too obviously badgered by the trade to be of any use, but the old lady in black satin who presided at the register looked fairly self-possessed. Her hands were flying through the work of sorting checks and punching keys as if they had a separate intelligent identity; her little sparrow eyes were busy with the room and had already noticed us, off in a huddle by ourselves, not patronizing the facilities. I sidled up to her and slipped my wallet open, not quite long enough to let her see exactly what it said there on the Photostat under the celluloid. "Excuse me, ma'am, was there some kind of trouble here a little while ago?"

The sparrow eyes were quizzically glittering at me behind rimless pince-nez. "The other officers took care of it."

"Oh, is that right? Somebody cutting up to where you had to call?"

"I didn't call you boys," she said disdainfully. She rang up half a dozen checks and kept on talking right along. "There wasn't anything the matter with the guest that I could see. He'd had a table by himself since breakfast and he must've been a little tipsy, I suppose, but not enough to bother anybody here. But when the officers came in to look around they didn't even ask me, they just took him out."

"You know these officers?"

"Why, no, I don't. They weren't the ones we usually have. They wouldn't even wait until the guest could pay his check. Of course we didn't mind so much this time, because he's staying here, so we can put it on the bill."

"Yes, ma'am. Could you describe these officers to me?"

She smoothly rang up thirty dollars' worth of business for an impatient waiter, counting out the change without a waver in the birdlike gleam behind her pince-nez. "Are you suggesting there was something wrong, young man?"

"No, ma'am, I'm not suggesting anything," I said. "I'd like an answer to my question, please."

"I really didn't notice much. The one who seemed to be in charge was quite an ordinary-looking person of about your age. He was much shorter, though, with rather long black hair, and nicely dressed for a policeman, just like you. He even wore a bow tie like the mayor, with those little polka dots."

The ice cubes in my stomach froze together in a ball. "You really didn't notice much," I quoted foolishly.

"The other one was bigger," she informed me calmly. "But I only saw his back."

The little woman had edged in beside me and was pulling at my sleeve. She clung to it while I plowed out into the street. The Pontiac's windshield still reflected the descending sun, and had been duly decorated with a yellow cardboard summons stuck between the wiper blades. I plucked it off without so much as grunting, put it in the glove compartment and slid in behind the wheel.

"Johnny, what does it *mean*?"

"It means I'll have to send the auto club a check for twenty bucks."

"Oh, darling, honestly! You know that isn't what I had in mind."

I pushed the dashboard lighter in and gave myself

a cigarette. "Max Ulrich wears a polka-dot bow
tie," I said. "It showed up clearly on his mug sheet,
and it's probably one of those little affectations
crooks go in for, and which cops will sometimes
overlook. He also happens to be shorter than I am.
His hair is black, and he's a snappy dresser, like the
man in Springfield says. Now *you* pick up a card."

"But what's he got against our client?" she
demanded in bewilderment.

"That's a good question, honey lamb. I think I
know the answer, but it doesn't help us very much.
Let's take it that the other J.P. Bundy actually was
a big-time fence. I've often told you how they
operate: they don't just sit and wait until somebody
rings the bell and offers them a suitcase load of
stolen merchandise for sale. They organize these
things by scouting in advance for stuff they figure
they can make a profit on. They hire the stealing
done, on shares, and generally through a middleman. A heavy-rackets guy like Maxie is to all intents
and purposes a subcontractor, who might never
meet the boss and might not even know his name.
The middleman would take delivery of what he
scored, and in due course would pay him off."

She frowned at me in concentration. "What
you're saying is that he might have mixed up our
Mr. Bundy with the one who died. But then why
would he want to kidnap him?"

"That part of it is not so difficult. This mail-truck
robbery was in the papers last September, I remember now. What must have happened was that Max
turned over the proceeds before he had to take it
on the lam to Mexico. The cops down there got on
his trail and shot it out with him, and dumped him
in the goldfish bowl for life. He'd blown a couple of

them down, but they abolished the garrote years ago. So he breaks out last week and makes it back to California, presumably without assistance from the fence or from the middleman, who must have figured that he wouldn't need his payoff anymore. Okay, we'll say that he does have the names and he finds out where Papa can collect. He makes a pass at Bundy Two last Tuesday night, but when the lights go on upstairs he thinks they may be phoning the cops, so he takes off and doesn't get to see the guy. What would be your next move, if you were in his shoes?''

''I wouldn't like to be,'' said Suzy seriously. ''I'd be happy just to stay away from trouble. But I might approach this middleman of yours.''

''And you'd be wrong. This middleman of mine, according to Dave Hogan, seems to be one Theodore 'Kicks' Henderson, who is a very hard boy in his own behalf. He runs a bowling alley on El Nido, just this side of Santa Monica, and probably has never even been arrested, but his rep says he's the greatest fixer in these parts since Bugsy Siegel bossed the syndicate out here. No, sir, if I were Max, I wouldn't tangle with him if it could be helped. I'd concentrate on Mr. Bundy, watch his place for a few days and see what gives. If I'd done that this week, I would've caught these ambulances going back and forth, including one from Shady Dell. They wouldn't have impressed me very much. I would've figured that it was a stall, arranged especially for my benefit. It would have seemed too pat, from where I stood, the guy just popping off like that within two days after I'd given him a scare. He'd know I'd be in no position to check into the details, and he would hope I might give up and go away. So I'd keep watching, and this morning, sure enough, this handsome chap comes calling who immediately spots my boy and hangs the brush on him. That smells like private dick to me.''

"What's good about that?" Suzy asked uncertainly.

"It's good, because I'm bound to figure it confirms the stall. It looks like Bundy knows I didn't fall for it, so now he's hired this dick to take me off his back. Which shows that he's afraid of me, and liable to skip his bail. That doesn't worry me a lot, because the dick can't do much to me, not and keep his client out of jail. But if I stick to him, he'll have to lead me back sometime to where the guy is hiding out.''

"You mean we led Max Ulrich to the Arizona Palms, and he found out there was a J.P. Bundy staying there, and simply collared him?''

"I know,'' I said. "It sounds preposterously brazen. But how else can you account for it? He obviously got the notion that this Bundy had been giving him the royal run-around. He and Bat Wiley wouldn't have much trouble posing as a pair of cops. They probably went up against the manager—I thought that desk clerk talked a little strange. And after all, it takes a bit of nerve to rob the mails.''

"But where were you while this was going on?'' demanded Suzy pointedly.

I told her where and why, and how the things I'd learned there only tended to confirm the deal. "This Baron lad is interested in a different way. Of course he didn't say so, but he thinks that Bundy left a cache of stuff somewhere, which is entirely possible, and that the Carstairs woman knows about it, which I doubt. So I'm supposed to tip him off on what her movements are the next few days, and I'm supposed to be too dumb to see the real reason why."

The sidelong glance she passed me held a thousand generations' worth of enigmatic female sympathy.

"We're in an awful situation, aren't we, darling? How do you consider we should tackle it?"

"I'll do the tackling, thank you just the same," I said. "This is one game where they're not hiring any girls to play. There's nothing for it but I'll have to brace this mob. The client can't expect to buy a lot of ethics for his hundred bucks, but even if I want to be a bastard and renege on him, the case itself is due to break out in the papers with a rash like poison oak. Then we could go and open a health-food store in Toronto, Canada."

"That sounds like fun," Suzy observed judiciously. "We'll do just that, right now. Unless."

"Now wait a minute, pussy cat...."

"For what? We've waited long enough. We've let them get a half-hour start on us."

"Listen, I can move faster and do better by myself! And I'm not about to get into a shooting match or anything. I've got a plan that ought to put it over nice and easy without anybody working up a sweat."

"Well, good!" she praised me lavishly, as if I were the dog and had just learned another trick. "That means I'll be quite safe in tagging after you."

I groaned convincingly, and said, "Now look. If you'll get out and go on home and let me handle this, I'll buy you a home freezer bigger than the one at Alice's."

"Oh, Johnny, will you, really? Full of steaks at ninety cents a pound?"

"They're ninety-eight, you said. And most of them are chuck or ground."

"That's right, they are. No, thank you, darling. Thank you very much. I'd rather have a husband, for investment purposes. A bigger one than Alice's, of course. I'd insist on that."

I let her see my helplessly frustrated grin. Next thing she'd bring that up again, about how Great-grandma Willet used to go for renegade Comanches with an ax.

BILL MARTIN, AT THE AUTO CLUB, gave me his customary grumble on the phone about these characters who never bothered him except when he was ready to go home. He wanted me to know that this was Saturday, and after four o'clock, and he'd been working overtime since noon. He asked me if I realized I was a lucky stiff to find him in. I said he'd be surprised what all I realized these days.

"You kidding? Me, surprised at anything, the job I got? You wanna try this for a week, and I'll take over from you in your racket. Anytime, pal, anytime at all. Okay, you got a pencil handy, here she blows. That's 2XB0994, a Plymouth light delivery. It's registered to Travelers U-Drive-It Company, Incorporated, 1690 Wilshire Boulevard, L.A. Think you can do with that, or do you want the motor number and the date of factory delivery, and maybe what the mileage was last time they changed the oil?"

8

THE TRAVELERS U-DRIVE-IT COMPANY proved to be quartered in the basement of a large and modern office building in downtown Los Angeles. Its entrance ramp sloped steeply from the street into a hollow rumbling cavern of concrete and cream-white plastic tile, illuminated by a battery of fluorescent daylight tubes. Its vast expanse of empty floor space looked as hygienic as a dairy plant's. The only transportation visible in there consisted of a single motor tricycle and one small yellow Datsun a young black in spotless coveralls was fondly lubricating on the hoist.

The manager wore horn-rimmed spectacles, a crisp camel's-hair sports jacket and a deferential smile. He issued from his glass-walled office cubicle the moment I pulled up, and wished us a good evening inquiringly. I said we'd like to talk with him, and he ran all the way around the car to help the little woman out and hold the door for us. The chromium and canvas chairs he offered would have graced a movie actor's dressing room.

I pushed my business card across the desk and he inspected it complacently enough. "We haven't scratched a fender in three weeks."

"This might be more expensive, and I doubt that

your insurance covers it," I said. "Mind looking up
the papers on your 2XB0994?"

"The panel job?" He seemed to be politely taken
by surprise. "What's wrong with it?"

"The car should be all right. The guy who rented
it from you would be an expert driver, I'm afraid."

He blinked at me and pulled a drawer of his filing
cabinet, dug out a gray manila envelope and
dumped its contents on the desk: the registration,
the insurance binder and his copy of the rental
contract, with a credit card slip clipped to it. He
thoughtfully removed the slip and studied it before
he passed the documents to me. "I haven't seen this
man myself," he said. "My night manager made
this rental early Thursday morning, for three
days."

"He mention to you people why he needed a
delivery van?"

"That's the only vehicle we've had available this
week," the manager said carefully. "We've got a
fleet of sixty passenger sedans, but every one of
them had been reserved by the convention transportation office long ago. It's been like that all over
town."

The contract form had been filled out by typewriter. The lessee's name was Joseph Randall Wiley
whose address was given as 4946 Live Oak Street in
St. Louis, Missouri, profession ladies' hosiery
salesman, holder of Missouri operator's license
number Y170081.

The credit card slip bore the same, on an Ameri-
can Express form. I'd have been amused if this had
not been such a common situation. Driver's licenses
and credit cards are stolen all the time, of course,
but your hard-line professional prefers to use his

own whenever he can possibly afford it. Never mind that he is not supposed to qualify for them. He handles it. "Your customer is a convicted felon and a fugitive," I said.

The manager looked glum. "Like that, is it?" he said. "I guess it's been some time. We get one maybe twice a year. Last June we had one used a spanner on his wife and ran the heap over a cliff with her behind the wheel. What's this one pulled, or should I ask?"

"He had to have a car for a few days that wasn't on the hot sheet, so he could afford to park in it," I said evasively. "If he comes in or calls, don't hesitate or tip him off in any way that something's going on. I'm sure that he'll return the vehicle. Just let him have his way, and we'll take over afterward."

"You gonna stick around? I go off duty here at six." He shot a doubtful glance at Suzy, who was calmly sitting by, demurely feminine in her new hairdo and her white cotton.

My watch said half-past four. "If you don't mind we'll wait and talk with your relief man," I suggested. "Then we'll have to try another tack."

The little woman said, "I wonder if you keep a record here of transient cars that have come in for servicing this week. We'd like to have some information on a Chevrolet with Texas license 4A413."

"We don't get many transients," said the manager. He found a ledger in the desk and ran a finger down its last few sheets and shook his head. "No Texas cars at all, the past ten days." He sounded less regretful than relieved.

I shrugged and wandered out to use the pay

phone on the wall outside. The gruffly irritable voice of Frank Brownell barked at me from six miles away over the background chatter of a children's television show. "Oh, so it's you. How'd you come out?"

"I haven't yet. The going got a little rough. But it looks like you had something last night."

"Damn right I did!" he crowed. "We checked this morning with the association, and they were about to close the file because the guy was dead. They had his last address, and nothing else on him to brag about. We tried to call your place, but you'd already left."

It would have been that simple, if I'd thought of it myself. I could have played his hunch and called the association office from my home. I could have called the Lord girl, written my report based on her story, sent it off by messenger to the hotel and spent the day collecting stamps or working in the yard. But not Professor Marshall—not as long as he could figure out a way to go about it where he'd wind up with a bunch of hoodlums, stolen diamonds, a blackmail case, a kidnapping and very possibly a killer on his hands.

The phone was crackling in my ear. "Hello! Can't hear a word you're saying, Johnny. Hold it, will you please?" He shouted at the kids off-mike, and the TV show faded to a mutter. "How was that again?"

"Just mumbling in my sleep," I said. "Look Frank, I need cooperation on this deal."

"What do you mean, cooperation? Don't we always back you up? Of course," he added cunningly, "you're not exactly working for the company on this."

"I hadn't planned to bill the company. I've got to

have a check for fifty grand. Can you run over to the office right away and make it out?''

The line fell silent for a long two seconds. I had pointed the receiver at the wall, but the big blast did not come off. Instead of that he sounded nervous and uncertain of himself. "Say, listen, Johnny, you okay? Just answer yes or no.''

"Sure, I'm okay.''

"Nobody with you who can hear?''

"Not at this end. Stop being cagey, will you, Frank? I'm only asking for a piece of paper, but I need it fast.''

He laughed uneasily. "Some piece of paper. Don't you know I couldn't even sign alone for that amount?''

"Of course I know. Just countersign it Zeke McGillicuddy or whatever comes to mind. It's not supposed to go through any bank. You'll get it back tomorrow if I don't put on a lot of sudden weight.''

"Where are you now?''

I told him where, and he quit hanging by his thumbs. "You'll never bring if off, whatever it's supposed to be.''

"That's right, I won't. Not if you don't get on the ball.''

He started to complain that he'd already put his slippers on, and I hung up on him. The manager was showing Suzy snapshots of his family. I ran the Pontiac off the ramp and backed it out of sight into a corner, just in case, and joined them in the office cubicle. The minutes started marching by like little sandwich men on stilts who carried signs that advertised the captivating charms of Shady Dell Memorial Park. They all had faces like my Uncle Ralph. I saw them clearly, every time I closed my eyes.

The call came in at 5:15.

We watched the manager while he was taking it. I was afraid he'd overplay his hand, but he appeared to be enjoying this somehow. He winked at us as soon as he'd identified the customer, and made his side of it sound briskly confident, with just a touch of faint vexation at the inconvenience. "Yes, sir. I see.... Well, yeah, we can, if you'll be busy. But you'll have to meet the lot boy when he makes the pickup, verify the mileage with him and sign out the contract.... Very well. As soon as we can make it." He replaced the phone, took off his glasses, peered at us nearsightedly and breathed a sigh. "Olympic and Descanso," he informed us. "At a service station on the northeast corner. That the way you wanted it?"

"Looks like he's nervous," I said. "Probably he'll wait across the street to see if there's a plant on him. Don't tell your man a thing except to take it very slow. We'll have to let him get a start, and it's not more than thirty blocks from here."

"You people better know your stuff," the manager said doubtfully. He shook his head and left the room. Outside, the three-wheeled motorcycle started with a hollow roar. It soon warmed up and puttered off sedately on the exit ramp.

We were already rolling after it when Frank Brownell's big Chrysler station wagon dived in through the entrance with a squeal of brakes.

THE JANUARY DUSK had gathered into early night, and traffic on Olympic Boulevard was like a solid stream of headlights racing west toward the ocean, east toward the city. The Descanso intersection was a minor one that did not even rate a traffic light. It was a neighborhood of former elegance, long since decayed. Two corner lots were vacant, deep in brush and weeds. A third had been improved some-time in Wilson's second term with a four-storied clapboard mansion carrying a gabled roof. The service station was an independent, recently re-modeled, brightly lighted. Its single three-pump island seemed to be quite sparsely patronized.

There was no sign of the green Plymouth van. The motor tricycle with the black lot boy in the saddle waited at the curb.

We were in a position to survey these things un-advertised and from a hundred yards away because Descanso, after it crosses the boulevard, funnels uphill into a dead-end barricade, and we had found a parking spot in the abandoned driveway of a private bungalow with a For Sale sign picketed into its lawn.

It was a cockeyed situation, not unlike a pair of mice watching a cathole, and I couldn't seem to make myself be pleased with it. We'd been finessed into a risky jog of straight police work, partly by the hapless chain of circumstances, partly by my own stupidity, and on its outcome was inevitably staked what little reputation I'd been able to build up in the profession for the past six years. We had ac-cepted risks before, and done police work when we couldn't help ourselves. But not for just a hundred bucks, and not against this kind of odds.

The dashboard radio was murmuring a Mendels-sohn concerto, turned down low. The noisy traffic river on Olympic was beginning to exhaust itself. All over town garage doors would be groaning shut and cocktail shakers would be rattling, and the smell of pot roast or fried chicken would be floating from a million kitchen stoves. The sultry desert wind had died at sunset, and the palm-tree fronds over our heads hung still. Suzy was shivering a little in her summer dress. I reached behind us for the Indian blanket on the rear seat and she wriggled into it. "Darling, you think he'll show?"

"Who knows? These lads are liable to be a trifle circumspect. They realize I'm on to them, of course, but they're not likely to be scared of any private operator, and they'll figure that the chances are against my calling in the cops just yet."

"Why would they bother to return this van at all?"

"Same reason why they rented it, and why Bat Wiley used a driver's license and a credit card in his own name," I said. "They needed transportation for three days, right here in town. It's easier to steal a car, and cheaper, but you wind up on computer tape in a few hours and on the squad-car hot sheets by next morning. When you can afford to, play it safe."

"They stole that Texas car," Suzy reminded me disdainfully.

"So it would seem. Presumably just for their kidnap caper at the Arizona. It'd have looked funny if they'd used the van for that."

The little men on stilts from Shady Dell went marching by again. This time I saw them only when I briefly let my eyes relax from focusing downhill across the boulevard. The palm fronds started rustling with the chilly ocean breeze that suddenly came puffing in. I set the heater switches, reached for the ignition key and changed my mind. A large black Buick Century came sliding down Olympic and turned north, between the service station and the clapboard house. It flicked its headlights on and crept along the block, as if prospecting for an unfamiliar address.

"Looks like our company," I said, and snapped the radio off.

The Buick turned west again at Ninth and disappeared from view. Two minutes later it returned and scrupulously halted for the boulevard stop, scurried through the intersection, crawled uphill toward the dead-end barrier. The headlights slowly brushed our windshield, caught what was behind it, caught the picket sign and swept along. When it came back, it probed the cottages across the street.

Suzy released me and leaned back against the seat. We were both breathing fairly fast, and she was looking at me rather oddly. "Well, indeed! I don't think I've been kissed like that in years."

"Not in a car, I hope. Or for an audience," I said, and watched the Buick swing left into the service station, pull up at the pumps and buy a load of gas. Almost immediately the moss-green Plymouth van made its appearance as it turned into Descanso two blocks south and rolled sedately up into a parking slot behind the rental office tricycle. Bat Wiley swung down from behind the wheel, allowed the lot boy to check his odometer, signed clipboard papers with a flourish and climbed into the black Buick.

I was in trouble right away, just catching up with him. He wasn't speeding, but he kept the needle on the legal limit, and the lights out here are staggered to allow just that, which means that missing one will spoil a tail job almost irretrievably. The Buick was hot, all right; its plates were local, with a white and green caduceus shield attached. Some for-

tunate M.D. in Glendale or in Sherman Oaks was
having dinner, blissfully unconscious of the empty
driveway in his yard. He'd probably be glad to offer
me another hundred dollars if I'd very kindly go
ahead and get his flivver back for him. I didn't feel
the slightest inclination to be kind. I didn't even
have a gun on me.

"This isn't going to work out," the little woman
said.

I grunted noncommittally, but privately had to
agree with her. The ice was very thin—it almost was
a cinch to crack. By daylight and in heavy traffic you
can sometimes get away with tailing seasoned crim-
inals, although the cops will always use two cars to
do it, and when I was in the C.I.C. in Germany we
never used fewer than three, with two-way radio,
twelve blocks or so apart. At night on high-speed
roads with little traffic it becomes a very tricky problem, even if you're organized to deal with it. Most
any time Bat Wiley would be noticing the same
bright headlights keeping pace with him. I had
already switched them twice, but if he caught me doing that it would be just as bad. He only had to make a
turn and run around the block to satisfy himself.

"We'll have to pitch to him," I said reluctantly.

The intersection lights at Fairfax Avenue were
straight ahead and turning red. The Buick slowed
down; I honked at it, and it politely veered aside to
let me pass. The driver had his window open and his
elbow out, but head and shoulders were in shadow.
For ten seconds we'd be rolling side by side in second gear. "This is where you can start appreciating
me," said Suzy cheerfully. She reached to touch the
jutting elbow. "Mr. Wiley, may we speak with you
a moment, please?"

The Buick jarred to a stop that killed its motor dead. I'd more or less expected that, and managed to pull up in line with it. The driver's head popped out as if it had been mounted on a spring and hidden in a box. It had a shrill, sarcastic voice, like a small buzz saw going through a trunk of sugar pine. "Hey, Sis, ya lost ya taffy? Watcha tryna do, put us on social security?"

He was a long-nosed, pimply-faced young kid who wore a mallard feather in the ribbon of his jaunty porkpie skimmer, and he was alone. The little woman flinched from him as if he'd pulled a razor on her. "Why, you're not...."

I almost laughed. Our quarry had bugged out on us. He'd made us, after all, and he'd dropped off and ducked, quite probably before the Buick ever left the service station. Up ahead the lights turned green. A truck came barreling along behind, discharged a horn blast at us and went rumbling by. The long-nosed youth stepped on the starter. I cut my front wheels sharply, edging in to where we would lock bumpers if he tried to move, and pointed at the supermarket parking lot across the street.

"In there, and take it slow!"

He leered at us, a leer of unmistakable obscenity. "Say, what is this, a pickup? Listen, Sis, ya look okay to me, but Mickey Kroll don't hafta pay for it."

"Don't waste it, sunshine," she advised him placidly. "Obey the man so he won't wreck your pretty car. This is a new routine, where *you* get paid for being nice."

I backed away for a few inches, gestured at the market lot again. The Buick slid past my bumper, hesitated briefly and turned in. The market was already closed; the lot was lighted only by reflection from the boulevard's big sodium arcs. We were abreast once more, right in the middle of the empty tarmac, like a collie herding in a fractious ram.

He had a gun, of course. They never seem to have the slightest difficulty laying hands on one. Its muzzle rested on his window frame and stared at us, impersonally interested.

"You won't need that, fellow," I said coldly.

"Whadda you think, Sis?"

"Oh, I suppose you do," said Suzy. "If it really makes you feel safer, Mr. Kroll. But we're not going to arrest you, we just want to talk to you."

"Yeah? What about?"

"We represent the underwriters on the Springfield diamonds."

"A lady snooper! Now ain't that a pipperoo." His chuckle had falsetto overtones like broken glass. "Ya made a nice big bobble, Sis. I never been to Springfield in my life."

"We think you know someone who has."

He seemed to be considering the point. "What if I did? Why should I tear him off for you?"

"Nobody's asking you to tear him off," I said. "We work for the insurance company, not for the cops."

The gun looked at my teeth. "Turn blue, Jack," snarled its owner. "This is strictly between me and Sis." The porkpie hat, the pimply face popped out again; the leer was still in evidence. "Okay, Sis, ante up."

"He means you promised he'd get paid for putting up with you," I said.

Suzy pretended to ignore me. "There'll be money,

Mr. Kroll,'' she said. ''Enough of it to interest you
and your friends. Please listen very carefully. We'd
like to see Max Ulrich, and we want to make an
offer for the diamonds. We know he is in town,
and that you are in touch with him, but we're not
sure that he can still deliver them. We're worried
about that, because we heard they were delivered
to the fence last year. We heard he doesn't know
the fence, and that the man he kidnapped at the
Arizona Palms this afternoon is just a tourist from
the Middle West, and not connected with the case
at all. Now, if we let you go and promise not to
follow you, will you agree to contact Max and tell
him what I've just told you?''

The idling engines of our cars sounded much
louder than before. The valves on mine were playing Verdi's ''Anvil Chorus,'' and the Buick's were
purring like a tiger with a stomachful of meat. The
long-nosed kid had pulled back into shadow, and
the dull-eyed muzzle of his .38 had disappeared
from sight.

''Ya hear an awful lot of stuff, Sis, don'tcha,
huh?''

They were sarcastic words, but they were spoken
dubiously, half uncertainly. The little woman dug
an elbow deep into my ribs and said, ''Let's understand each other—Mickey. We're investigators, but
we're looking for a deal, not for an argument. I
wouldn't be here if we were, and you'd be riding in
a very different kind of buggy, don't you think?''

''Flat on his back,'' I mentioned nastily.

He didn't even hear me, he was so intrigued with
her and with the proposition. ''How much cush ya
gotta blow?''

She glanced at me inquiringly. ''He's asking you

for the amount we have been authorized to spend,"
I said.

"As much as necessary," she said firmly. "Within
reason. You tell Max exactly that."

"I never hearda him." He nonchalantly kicked
the Buick's accelerator, just to make a noise. "Why
don'tcha go and see a pitcher, Sis?"

"What picture—Mickey? Any special one you
recommend?"

"Nah, I don't care. They got one at the Skyland,
down on Centinela. Suit yaself." He started jockey-
ing away in slow reverse. "Just try and lay the flue
on us!" he snarled at her. The Buick jumped clear
and hit the boulevard in second, going fifty miles an
hour. Its rear lights were two crimson pin points
half a mile away before I'd even turned around.

"Well, that makes three of them," I said. "Nice
lad. Looks like you made a conquest, cherry pie."

Her hand was not quite steady, fumbling for a
cigarette. "He's just a little boy."

We were already rolling west again. She watched
me quietly, huddled in her blanket, though the
heater had been going since we'd left our stakeout
on Descanso Street. "I don't like trapping children,
even when they're bad," she said at last.

"This one would like to trap you, if he got the
chance."

"I know he would."

"Want me to take you home?" I asked her hope-
fully.

She smiled and shook her head. "I want to be
with you. No matter what you've got to do."

9

THE SKYLAND was a drive-in, rather small and old, located on the borderline between a district zoned for factory development in the southwestern part of town and its attendant residential neighborhood. It was a little after eight when we passed by the ticket seller's booth and let an usher's flashlight guide us to a parking slot on the third audience ramp, next to the center aisle.

I turned the loudspeaker attachment down as far as it would go. The previews were still showing, and the theater's wide sloping shell looked to be mostly empty space. The screen's detached and gaudy flicker had a ghostly quality. The savor of hot popcorn drifting by might have reminded me that dinner was considerably overdue, if it had not been tainted with the reek of crankcase drippings on concrete.

Suzy was stirring restlessly beside me. "Why do you suppose they sent us here?"

"Checkpoint," I said. "We may be forced to keep this up all night and go through many more, if they decide to take us on. It's up to them from here on in. They know the Feds are after them, of course."

"But how do they expect to find us in this place? There are at least two hundred cars already here, and more keep coming in."

"They'll find us if they want us, honey lamb. These people make a living at this. They'd be smart enough to make good cops themselves, just as there are a lot of cops who'd make good crooks. It's all a matter of whose team you happen to be on, sometimes."

The feature started rolling, one of those low-budget European costume epics with a lot of phony battles and elaborate seductions. I sat back and made myself relax and look at it, and even turned the speaker up. The sound track was a little less discordant than the drunken squabble in the pickup truck that flanked us on our right, and less distracting than the high-school sex party in the wide open hot rod on our left. Time passed, more slowly still than it had passed before. "Johnny, they wouldn't really hurt our Mr. Bundy, would they?"

"I'm afraid they would, if he were sober. As it is, they'll almost have to let him sleep it off. If he starts talking it won't make much sense to them, and they'll just figure he's still carrying a load. They haven't had much opportunity to mess around with him so far."

"Why not? It's been four hours."

"They're being forced to spend a lot of time and energy on other things. You'd be surprised how complicated life can get for thieves with loot for sale. And now we've pitched another curve they can't ignore."

The screen brought forth a black-haired beauty in a low-cut gown of scarlet Spanish lace and flourishing a black snakewhip. I couldn't quite make out if she intended to defend her honor with it or to punish the captain for leaving it intact. The sound

track failed to clarify the point. *I'll teach you manners, you—you swine....*

"Excuse me, sir, you Dr. Marshall, please?"

I winced as if the whiplash had been aimed at me,
and jerked around. The girl who stood beside my
window was a skinny, freckled blonde who looked
like she was freezing in her short shorts and glitter
top. She bore a candy tray suspended by a heavy
bandoleer from her emaciated little neck, and she
was studying a pencil note that had been scribbled
on the inside of a matchbook cover. "Pontiac '79,
6N9908. That's you, ain't it?"

*I'll never let you touch me. Never, do you
hear...!*

Suzy leaned over and turned down the speaker. I
said I was Dr. Marshall and the candy girl informed
me that the hospital had called and wanted me to
call it back. "Which hospital?"

She stared at me, confused. I dropped a dollar on
her tray and asked about the nearest phone. She
pointed out a battery of public booths under a shad-
ed spotlight off the exit ramp, a hundred yards
away.

I hit the starter and shoved off. The phone in
number one rang briskly when we stopped beside it
and squeezed in. Bat Wiley's hoarsely feral bass
came grating at my ear. "We make you clean, so
far."

"Don't strain yourself," I said. "I'm clean all
right."

"Go east on Centinela," he instructed me succinctly and hung up.

Suzy said uncertainly, "They must be watching
pretty close."

"There's probably a dozen spots from which

these phones can be observed. Let's get a move on, or they'll think we made another call.''

The Skyland shopping district still showed lights from drugstore windows, poolrooms, coffeepots and filling stations, but beyond, the highway narrowed, dipped across a shallow ridge and plunged into a murky no-man's-land of lumber yards and warehouse sheds toward the oil-well-studded hills of Baldwin Park. We traveled it for miles and seemed to have it strictly to ourselves. The moon was rising like a smoky orange, just a hand's breadth high above the distant city's sallow nimbus; somewhere overhead the mournful whistle of a landing jet shrieked by and died away. It was a nice long lonesome road, and built to order for a quick neat job of knocking off a couple of foolhardy people whom you might not care to trust.

"Johnny, how'd they find out our name?"

I tapped the steering column, where a cellophane-and-leather strap displayed the registration card. "They cased the deal this morning while I visited Miss Lord. That's how they know there is no two-way radio or any other signaling equipment in this car. And they've had time to check the grapevine, which is pretty sure to have confirmed that we do plenty of insurance work.''

She snuggled up to me as if we were some twelve years younger, and on our way home from the big college prom. "Darling, how sweet of you. You did say *we*. . . .''

A pair of headlights blazed up in my driving mirror and closed in on us at eighty miles an hour. I tensed instinctively when the black Buick came sizzling by and cut in front of me. But it kept going, and the driver's arm showed briefly through the window in a peremptory forward sweep. In Baldwin Park it coasted quietly through a speed zone, punctually made the boulevard stop at La Brea, then started burning up its rubber on the canyon freeway that swung north across the hills.

I kept my weight on the accelerator and just barely managed to stay with it for the course. At Santa Clara it slowed down at last, turned east again and rolled sedately on into the unincorporated city sector known as Crenshaw Heights. Here there was traffic once again, and sidewalks crowded with pedestrians, and lighted store fronts, and a hundred blocks of pastel stucco cottages on palm-tree-skirted streets. The Buick ignored them and kept going, crossed the railroad tracks and pulled into the driveway of a small red brick apartment house three blocks beyond.

"That does it, Jack."

The boy had popped up from the shadows of a giant sycamore that graced the building's front lawn of Bermuda grass. We were already in the driveway, and the Buick had disappeared around the corner of the service porch. I stopped and let him reach in through the offside window, punch the glove compartment lock and feel around inside. He snapped it shut, picked up the little woman's pocketbook and weighed it casually in his hand before he dropped it back into her lap. "Ya hungry, Sis?"

He pointed at the flashing blue-and-white electric sign across the street. The sign said Club Tahiti, *Dinner in the Tropics*, Driftwood Bar.

We stared at him. He opened Suzy's door and swept his porkpie skimmer off in an exaggerated bow. She smiled for him a little doubtfully, and slipped out on the lawn. "You, too, Jack. Leave the key. I'll park the heap for ya."

I shrugged in resignation and got out. He came around behind me, ran his hands under my arms and slapped my pockets and my belt. I had been frisked by crooks before, but it took self-control to keep from turning this one over on my knee. He smelled of hair oil, musk and poorly ventilated sweat. The flaxy stubble on his chin grew out almost an inch, and had been waxed into a small goatee.

He sneered at me and got behind the wheel, and spurted up the driveway. Suzy had grabbed my arm and was already dragging me toward the sign. It perched above a narrow entrance masked with rope and canvas like the gangplank of an ocean liner; inside there was artificial torchlight flicker, and the hollow-domed capaciousness of a large Quonset barn. The small Hawaiian orchestra sat on a bamboo raft and drifted slowly back and forth across the oval pool that used up half the floor space of the joint. The plaintive twang of steel guitars hung quivering in the musty air.

The tiny dance floor, separated from the pool by ship's taffrails, was packed with customers. The blues of sailors from the Long Beach naval base were mixed with Filipino ice-cream suits, and with the leisure wear of aircraft workers from the Northrop and McDonnell Douglas plants. A slender Chinese girl in black pajamas stiff with gold embroidery came up to meet us and impassively conducted us into a bamboo booth with imitation teakwood seats and screens of tapa cloth.

She had a set of menus, and stood by without a word while we attempted to decipher them in the uncertain light. I half presumed to find boiled leg of missionary listed, but we had to settle for chow mein and spareribs from the barbecue.

"Johnny, this must be it!"

"It's possible," I said. "Don't be surprised if they decide to drop us on our heads, right here. We're breaking all the rules for business transactions of this kind, and breaking them with heavy Joes who are already fighting with their backs against the wall. I wouldn't even have considered playing it this way if you had let me tackle them alone."

She put both elbows on the table, cupped her stubborn little chin. Her eyes were silver gray and very sober, searching mine. "You really think I've been a handicap to you?"

"It's not that simple, baby doll. Of course we've taken chances many times before, together, when we had to, and there is no question that you've ever let me down. But in this case there was no need for you to take a chance. When you insisted anyway, that meant you forced me to adopt a certain method of approach. No one can tell if there's a handicap in that or not, until we see how it works out."

"I know," she said. "I wanted you to try this method all the time. What's wrong with it? How are we breaking rules?"

I glanced around. The two adjoining booths were occupied by sailors with their girl friends, in a fairly noisy mood. "There's nothing wrong with it," I said. "This sort of show goes on quite often, and I've had a hand in some of them myself. But you're supposed to wait until the heat is off, and you're supposed to use their mouthpiece for a contact man instead of bracing them yourself. You're *not* supposed to bait them with a phony offer to negotiate,

and plan to welsh on them as soon as they release
your client, after you've convinced them that they
made a slight mistake in snatching him. They're
likely to resent you if you're not sincere with them.
Of course in this case they're not very likely to find
out about it, and the Feds are bound to kick them
over pretty soon. But you were asking me how
we've been breaking rules.''

"Oh, is that all?"

She made it sound as if we were discussing how
much money we should spend for groceries next
week. I shook my head and looked around some
more. The Chinese waitress was arriving with our
tray. The orchestra had disembarked; the bamboo
raft lay moored under its lacquered canvas
baldachin. The torches on the walls had dimmed,
and somewhere in the building's dome flashed up a
bolt of artificial lightning followed by the customary booming stage effects. Rain from the
sprinkler system started hissing on the surface of
the pool, not loud enough to drown the Club
Tahiti's steady din of muddled revelry.

The food was good. It almost always is in places
where the Navy trades. We were just digging into it
when from the crowd around the bar a man detached himself who crossed the now deserted dance
floor and came up the aisle toward our booth,
unhurriedly, as if he thought he didn't need the
exercise. Without formality he slid into the corner
seat that faced me, next to Suzy, who moved over
to make room for him—more room, more quickly,
than convention would have urged.

For fully half a minute no one said a word. We
went on eating, and he seemed content to watch us
at it, in the same completely neutral spirit as that of

a total stranger watching laborers tear up the pavement of a street. I had a little trouble recognizing him at all—the polka-dot bow tie was there, and he was pretty spruce in dark blue flannel with a tiny pinstripe, but he'd dyed his hair an ashen shade of blond and wore a set of horn-rimmed spectacles, the kind with heavy temples that distort the facial contours. The medium complexion specified in his description had acquired a ruddy tan.

When he spoke up at last, his diction was precise, like an accountant's or a teacher's, and his nasal voice proved to be pitched almost uncomfortably high.

"So now you people want to make a deal!"

I put my fork down, took a sip of tea and looked at him. His smooth round features were completely blank, although the question seemed to indicate he was provoked with us somehow. "If you're in a position for it, yes," I said. "If not, somebody else may be."

He took his glasses off and cleaned them with a paper napkin, held them up against the light and put them on again. His eyes were olive brown, and glittered with suspiciousness. "If *I'm* in a position, did you say?"

"Well, are you? And don't tell me you expect to get the merchandise out of this dizzy Joe from Kokomo you're sitting on. We checked on him before we ever got around to you."

"You people got around to me in Vera Cruz," he mentioned frigidly. "That's when you claimed *you* were in no position to make deals."

The orchestra struck up "Waikiki Moon"; the barman had turned off our thunder squall. "This isn't Mexico," I said. "You're not in college now, and we're not offering to keep you out of it. It's not our job to catch you, either, but if you get sneezed again, we don't propose to hold back evidence or to abstain from prosecuting you. You stung the underwriters for five hundred coarse ones, Max. They want to cut the loss, is all. That doesn't mean they're willing to compound a felony.''

He took his eyes off me and turned them on the little woman, who'd continued nibbling daintily on her chow mein. I was reminded that his mug sheet had referred to him as being fond of female company. It was a faculty he seemed well able to control. "How'd you make out I was in town?"

"You've got your racket, Mr. Ulrich," Suzy told him dulcetly. "Why worry about ours?"

I started gnawing on a sparerib to disguise the twitch around my lips. I had quit worrying myself about the situation, since it was now fairly obvious that we were in with lots of room to spare. Unlike most crooks, this man was not a fool. But he had overspecialized and seemed to have acquired a kind of mental tunnel vision that had blinded him to anything not instantly within the scope of his activities. This blindness in itself is typical of many "heavy" felons, and will often make it possible to trip them up, by means that never would take in a grifter or a small-time thief.

"The fence," I said. "We've kept an eye on him for years. He's dead, my friend, in case you weren't aware of it. He broke his leg last Tuesday night when you were picking daisies in his backyard and he came to make a fuss about it with a gun. The marrow fat got to his lungs and pushed him off; they planted him on Friday up at Shady Dell. This other guy is just a tourist hick who doesn't have a thing to do with it.''

Max Ulrich wasn't even looking at us anymore. "What other guy?" he carelessly inquired.

"We think you know."

"Listen, you people say you want to make a deal, is why I'm here. Okay, I'll split the score with you, if you can put your chips into the pot tonight."

"Let's get this straight," I said. "You claim you've actually got the Springfield touch in hand? You didn't turn it over to the fence?" He shrugged almost disinterestedly and started polishing his spectacles again.

Suzy said earnestly, "But Mr. Ulrich, don't you see, we have a right to ask. . . ."

I moved my plate aside and lighted a cigarette, as slowly as it could be done without appearing like a stall. I wasn't happy anymore—he'd read a line for us that shouldn't have been in the script. There were at least a dozen solid reasons why he couldn't possibly come up with any diamonds tonight, if he could ever manage to come up with them at all.

"He wants to split the score," I said, and made it sound affectionately scornful. "Two hundred and fifty thousand dollars' worth. Maybe we ought to start this at the other end. The bid is ten, and not another cent. That would be C.O.D., of course. Tonight or any other night."

The blank-faced man in the blue pinstripe shrugged again and rose to leave. That was all right—we'd made our point, I thought. He couldn't really be there to sell, no more than we were there to buy. The only thing he should be interested in was finding out he'd made a boner at the Arizona Palms that afternoon.

The little woman frowned at me uncertainly. Somehow I wasn't satisfied with it myself. It had been easy—possibly too easy—and I didn't like that one peculiar line of his. I wondered if the job might need more work. It's dangerous sometimes to try for extra tricks, but I was strongly tempted to indulge. Sometimes those extra tricks make all the difference.

"Why go off mad?" I said. "You're not just shopping, are you, Max? If you're all set to do a little business tonight, where else can you expect to get a price?"

He had already turned away. I was surprised to see him hesitate and swing around. "Ten G's is the reward you people have been offering since last September," he reminded me impassively.

"But Mr. Ulrich—not to you!" the little woman pointed out.

"He's right, of course," I said. "He doesn't have to work for the reward. Ten G's is only talking money anyway, for talking diamonds. The real article would be worth more than that to both of us. It might be worth as much as he'd been promised by the fence."

The blank-faced man sat down again. He put his small white pudgy hands palms downward on the table and proceeded to inspect his manicure. It was a gesture bordering on the effeminate, and I was forced to make myself remember that he was a coldly vicious ruffian, after all, who had committed any number of armed holdups, killed two Mexican policemen, and was holding my own client captive in his hideout, probably a cabin in some cheap motel.

"How much you people figure for your end?"

That made another line that didn't sound in character. He'd been suspecting us of haggling for a kickback, and there was no sense in that unless he genuinely wanted to go through with this. It would have been a serious mistake to take him up on the idea, or even to pretend at it. Most crooks have very funny ethics, strongly disapproving of dishonesty in those who are employed to deal with them. If they can bribe you they don't trust you, and the one thing we were interested in was Maxie Ulrich's confidence.

"If that's what's eating you," I said, "there's nothing I can do except to show you all the cards, my friend."

The fifty-thousand-dollar check was in a yellow office envelope. He took his glasses off and watched me like a terrier while I removed it from the inside pocket of my coat. There wasn't any doubt that Frank Brownell had done a handsome job of forgery. It was a pretty piece of paper, crisp and pink, and executed with a check-protector punch, a typewriter and two bold signatures, impressively illegible and drawn with different pens.

I put it on the table, threw a napkin over it and let him play with it. His smoothly vacant features did not even twitch, although the pudgy little hands weren't quite so steady anymore. When he glanced up at last, the glitter in his eyes had faded down to pinpoint size.

"You people know this guy who came to see me in the can at Vera Cruz?"

I shook my head. It was a curve ball, but it went so wide I didn't really have to look at it. "He would've been a Lloyd's man from Chicago, or perhaps from San Antonio," I said. "This check reads Mutual Indemnity because we carry most of their adjustments here in California."

He put the napkin over it again and pushed it back to me. "The price is right," he told me listlessly.

I knew it was for him. If we'd been actually trying to do business with him, I would've had to spend the evening on bargaining him down. A wholesale lot of unset diamonds which has been valued at $500,000 may be worth from two to three times that amount at retail, but the thief who gets his hands on it is lucky if he draws a take of ten percent. The finger man sees even less; it is the fixer and the fence who carve the melon like executives. They are, in fact, exactly that; they must provide the capital, the contacts and the market place.

"No kickback," I said carefully. "No fuss, no pinch, no grief of any kind. This paper is made out to me, of course, but there are half a dozen places where it can be cashed tonight. You bring the liquor, Max—I'll bring the girls."

He started to shove off again. I suddenly became aware that there was something wrong with him. It took me quite a little time to recognize it—all the time he needed to swing out his legs into the aisle and put his hands down on the table to stand up erect. His vacant features had been rearranged somehow, the lips drawn back into a grimace that displayed a set of chalk-white dentures and a badly coated tongue that licked their cutting edge. "You people have a phone," he snapped at us. "Pick up your chips and stay with it." He swiveled on his heels and strutted briskly past the pool's taffrail, pushed through the dancers on the floor and disappeared from sight.

10

"THERE GOES YOUR FREEZER, honey lamb," I said.

Suzy was thoughtfully consulting with her compact mirror, and repairing the minor damages. "He's got them, hasn't he?" she diagnosed composedly.

"He knows where he can get his hands on them within the next few hours, would be my guess. If he'd already had them in his pocket, he'd have offered taking us in tow. No use in going through that decontamination business again."

"But Johnny, I don't understand. If he knows where they are, it means he never lost possession of them, doesn't it? It means he must've hidden them somewhere before he fled to Mexico? Because if he had turned them over at the time, they'd surely have been sold by now."

"Not necessarily. It's only been four months or so."

"You think we're in a jam?"

I showed her my unruffled grin, and said, "Oh, not too bad. Maybe no worse than just a little bitty jam, like getting shot or having somebody hook up a stick of dynamite to the ignition of our car. The irony of it is that we've been taking all this trouble needlessly, because the client should be either safe or dead by now."

There was another possibility that had occurred to me, but it was such a crazy one I couldn't waste my time to play with it. There were too many other, much more urgent question marks to be eliminated first.

"Of course he's safe," the little woman said. "Why would they hurt him if they never lost the diamonds? Why did they kidnap him at all?"

I shrugged and said, "Let's face it; we don't know. We had a bright idea before, and it turned right around on us and laid a bomb. The way this thing is stacked just now, we've got a kind of hangman's choice. We either run for cover, whether it's to Dave or to the Feds, and take a roasting that'll last us for the next ten years. Or we stick out our necks, all the way out to there, and try to wrap it up ourselves."

She dropped her lipstick in her bag and snapped her compact shut. "I'll quit," she told me coolly. "If you'll quit."

"Ten grand and glory, or a drawer in the morgue," I said. "What *is* the matter with you, bright eyes, don't you like to live?"

"Yes, darling—very much. But not alone, and not the kind of life where I'd be just a pair of handcuffs and a ball-and-chain to you. I know you well enough to realize you want to solve this case so badly you can taste it, and you've obviously got another plan. It wouldn't make much sense for me to spoil it all by getting scared. And I'd be missing all the fun."

I had another plan, all right. A rodeo performer has a plan when he climbs on the back of a wild Brahma bull and swings his hat while he goes down the chute into the ring.

We might not even have the time to swing our
hats. I crooked a finger at the Chinese waitress,
fretting at the lazy elegance of her approach. She
had a properly inscrutable expression for us, but
she didn't have a check. "The other gentleman took
care of it," she languidly enlightened us.

I winced and started scrambling to my feet, but
Suzy was already halfway to the Club Tahiti's exit
gangway when I managed to catch up with her.

Behind us they were turning on the thunderstorm
effects again.

THE BRISTOL RECREATION CENTER on El Nido used to
be a country club. Now pink neon contoured its
gabled roof and writhed aloft from it to spell out

16 Bowling Alleys 16

in Old English script. Its rolling grounds had long
ago been subdivided into building lots and covered
with a rash of shingle, frame and stucco, but the ancient flagstone clubhouse still remained, surround-
ed by the eighteenth green's original and stately
eucalyptus grove.

We left the Pontiac at the curb on Carmelita,
round the corner and across the city line. It had
been meekly waiting for us in a carport stall in the
backyard of the apartment house in Crenshaw
Heights where Mickey Kroll had intercepted us, and
its ignition system had been innocent of foreign
wires attached to detonator caps. We'd made the
fifteen miles into the outskirts of the beach resort
of Santa Monica in twenty minutes flat. My wristwatch said 9:40 when we walked into the lobby of
Kicks Henderson's domain.

The lobby was pink glazed concrete and strictly functional. A one-chair barbershop, a shoeshine parlor and a newsstand were still doing business; the pinball battery was clicking merrily away. The snack bar had a waiting list, and filled the premises with the hot spicy redolence of frying meat. A jukebox was dispensing rock with all the power of its brassy electronic lungs. It could not quite compete in volume with the turbulently repercussive wooden pulse beat of the bowling balls. The sign above the rental and equipment counter proudly boasted Anyone Who Enjoys Work Can Have A Hell of a Good Time in This Establishment.

There were at least a hundred patrons lounging in the bleachers, and the 16 Alleys 16 were all occupied. They seemed to have been crammed into the country club's old banquet room. Pink draperies concealed the row of former casement arches, now cemented up, where dining members and their guests had once looked out upon the sweep of fairways and the velvet carpet of the greens; a scuffed and mottled stretch of parquet floor remained intact under the bleacher seats. The little woman took my arm and looked about in mild surprise. "It has a lot of atmosphere," she said. "But not the kind one would expect, somehow. You're sure this is the place?"

I laughed at her and marched her off toward the left, where the old staircase to the locker rooms descended past a painted arrow indicating Sammy's Strike'n'Spare. "He doesn't know it, but it happens Kicks and I are practically bosom pals," I said. "Two years ago his home in Pasadena burned, and Mutual was on it for a nice big policy. The fire department experts called it arson, which it was, except he didn't have a thing to do with it. He's not that kind of crook at all.''

"You mean you caught the firebug for him, just like that?''

I shook my head and said, "The fire department did. But that was six weeks later, when he tried again, next door. It was the milkman, and he was a psychopath. The point is I checked up on Kicks and recommended payment of his claim. He's not supposed to be aware of it, of course.''

There was a second jukebox in a corner of the Strike'n'Spare. It played a disco medley for the benefit of six or seven couples on the tiny dance floor and a dozen more who were discreetly parked at widely separated tables under artificial candlelight. The barman was a wrinkled oldster who appeared to be engrossed in matching pennies with his only customer, a husky middleweight in dinner jacket who looked up to listen to me asking for the boss. "Mister, that's me, down here. You got a beef?''

"Not yet,'' I said.

The husky turned around and stared at us. He would have been a handsome lad but for the gray, unhealthy pallor of his skin that spoke of stomach trouble, and the puckered scar that ran for inches down the outline of his jaw. The drink before him in a tumbler had a milky shade and looked more like a carminative than an intoxicant. "What's on your mind?'' he asked me, flatly unconcerned.

"I doubt if Mr. Henderson would like me to discuss that here,'' I said.

He cocked an eyebrow for me, pushed his stack of pennies over on the bar and slid down off his stool to disappear behind a screen of corrugated glass that flanked the stairs. A door slammed shut as if it never would be used again. The barman started polishing mahogany with a clean scrap of cloth. "Mister, I wouldn't pick on Steve if I was you," he counseled.

"Oh, wouldn't you? What's he dressed up for in a joint like this?"

"He's got a date," the barman said, and smacked his lips as if he couldn't stand the thought. "She works at Paramount tonight, is why he's waiting for her to call up and tell him when she's through."

"I hope she's kept herself in training," said the little woman soberly.

The barman glanced at her. "Steve's a good boy," he said. "He just don't seem to have no sensayuma, is what's wrong with him. A man should ought to have a sensayuma, if he's gonna get along and don't want people picking on him, is the way I figure it."

The door that had been slammed for keeps burst open after all. The gray-faced husky came around the screen to scowl at us and jerk a thumb. We followed it down a short corridor still paved in tiled concrete. Behind the door a coarse pink broadloom rug covered the tiles, but very little else had been provided to remodel what was left of the old locker room. They had put up some wallboard and moved in a set of standard office furniture in walnut-painted steel and yellow leatherette. Kicks Henderson was lounging in a swivel chair, both feet in beaded Indian moccasins on the desk. He looked relaxed and cheerful, and as big as city hall, just sitting there and grinning at us like a politician on election day. His nose was big, his mouth was big, his jowls were big, his grizzled lion's mane of hair was big. The highball glass he held, a sixteen-

ouncer, almost vanished in his huge red paw; the
Racing Form he'd been consulting seemed reduced
to postcard size. He wore his working clothes, the
wardrobe he'd adopted thirty years ago when he'd
been one of Willie Bioff's studio-labor racketers—
the tawny flannel slacks, horse-blanket shirt and
coat of bottle-green suede. He was a sportsman and
a gentleman of parts who wouldn't harm a fly as
long as it agreed to help him sell another glass of
beer.

His booming welcome had a carny barker's ring of
hospitality. "Howdy thar, folks, how are ya? Step
right up'n'say hello.... What was the name
again?" He saw us looking at his feet and swung
them to the floor but did not bother to get up. My
card removed the grin as if I'd rubbed a towel over
it. "Hey, Steve, you got no manners? Little lady
needs a chair." He drained his highball at a gulp and
put the glass down with a bang that shook the desk.
"You look familiar to me, pal," he snapped at me.

"I do?"

"Sure, you was here before." He crooked a
finger, flicked my card clear off the desk. I noticed
then I'd given him one of the kind with just my
name on it. "Them highway robbers," he boomed
angrily. "Sixty-five grand they charge me for
depreciation on my property, after they put a
snooper on me for a couple days to see can they get
out of paying me a cent. You didn't figure I was
wise to you, huh, snooper?" he inquired of me.

"I wasn't worrying about it, Mr. Henderson," I
said. "There's no such thing as an insurance company that will pay off on a large policy without first
making a routine investigation like I made on you.
But if you really feel that Mutual's adjustment was

unfair, that time, you'll have a very pretty chance
to reimburse yourself tonight.''

Steve came around the desk and roughly elbowed
past me to pick up the card and drop it in a metal
basket with the other trash. He carefully took
off his dinner jacket and revealed a pigskin shoulder strap that held a sawed-off Luger pistol in
its clip. He hung the jacket on a chair, removed the
strap and put it with the gun still in it on the
desk. He started rolling up his shirt sleeves, neatly,
so they wouldn't wrinkle very much. The muscles
on his forearms were a sight to see. He flexed
them once or twice like a mechanic testing out his
tools, and turned to look me over, rather sullenly,
as if resenting me for putting him to all this inconvenience. ''You want it standing up or lying
down?''

I looked him over in agreeable disdain. He was
about three inches shorter, and I had some thirty
fairly solid pounds on him, but even with that
stomach ulcer he could probably give me a nasty
workout if he tried. ''Some other time,'' I said.
''Relax, champ, will you please? I'm here to raise a
little money, not a lot of dust.''

He sneered at me and feinted with his left before
he swung the roundhouse right that was supposed
to knock me for a loop. I blocked the feint and
ducked his Sunday punch by squatting on my heels
to grab his ankle, push him gently in the belly and
upset him on his back. He hit the rug a little harder
than I'd meant him to. It took him a few seconds to
get back his breath and overcome the big surprise.
He scrambled to his feet at last, and started shuffling over to me in a fighter's crouch.

I sighed in resignation and got set for him. Suzy

said disapprovingly, "Why don't you children run along and play outside?"

Behind the desk Kicks Henderson broke out in a terrific, crashing guffaw of a laugh. Steve glanced at him in sour disgust and straightened up to turn his back on me. He started rolling down his sleeves again. I settled comfortably in a chair and said, "Okay, you guys have fun—it's all the same to me. I told you we dropped by to spend a chunk of dough. But you can talk me out of it."

Steve made the usual impractical suggestion in a flat, unpleasant undertone. The big man in the swivel chair stopped laughing. "Watch the mouth," he ordered wrathfully.

"But Chief, this snooper's feeding us the sting...."

"That don't excuse you with the little lady. Go ahead, apologize."

The gray-faced man was strapping on his shoulder clip. He froze in that position, slightly hunched, one hand still on the buckle clasp under his arm. "Who, me?"

"Oh, honestly!" said Suzy, smiling in exasperated tolerance.

That seemed to close the incident. I had already tossed the envelope with Frank Brownell's impressive slice of rubber on the desk, and Kicks was holding it at arm's length, peering at it with an air of fatuously quizzical astonishment. "The company would like to have a little help from you," I said.

He let the check drop on his blotter, but he couldn't keep his gaze off it. "For that they can buy lots of help," he said. "Why pick on me? Besides, this thing's made out to you, ain't it?"

"I'll get it cashed or I'll endorse it, any way you

want. But most of it is not for you. It all depends upon what kind of bargain you can make for us."

His hearty chuckle rattled off the walls. "Is that a fact? You fellows ain't so bad at making bargains for yaself. I found that out last year." He reached into a drawer and produced more highball tumblers and a quart of I.W. Harper, nearly full. "Well, now, maybe we ought to do this right," he said. "Maybe what I'm forgetting is me sacred duties as a host."

He poured three drinks and glanced at Steve, who leaned against the wall and gestured glumly in refusal. "It's like this," I said. "The deal we're looking for is one we're not in a position to put through ourselves. We're hoping you can manage it somehow. You're known to have connections, Mr. Henderson, and we're inclined to trust you fully in this matter and to let you work it out the way you think is best. The bargaining of it would be entirely up to you—you've got the figure we're prepared to make available before you there. Of course your own commission will have to come out of that."

He tossed his triple premium bourbon down the hatch as if it were a Coke, and watched me sipping mine. His jowls were still aquiver with amusement, but cupidity gleamed in his bulging bulldog eyes. "What're you after, pal?"

"We heard that Max the Dude's in town."

"Who's he?"

I rose, put down my drink, picked up the check and slipped it back into its envelope. "If you don't know, we may as well forget it," I said cheerfully. "Some other time, perhaps. It's getting late, and there are two more contacts we're supposed to make on this tonight."

The gray-faced man said, "Chief, I'm warning ya. He's feeding it to us for sure."

That seemed to be the wrong psychology. Kicks reached across the desk and snatched the envelope out of my hand. He made another careful scrutiny of its contents. "Whyn't you fellows have this certified?"

I could have told him, truthfully enough, that it had been made out long after banking hours, but I decided to ignore the point. He splashed another slug into his glass and slapped a heavy ballpoint pen in front of me. "Write out 'Value received' and put down your John Hancock," he instructed me.

"What do you want?" I asked him. "Eat your cake and have the crumbs in bed with you?"

He threw his massive head back and exploded in another guffaw. Then he downed his drink and glared at me through beetled brows. "The Springfield job," he said, as calmly as a preacher saying grace.

I shrugged and took his pen and started to endorse the check. It was the only thing to do; I understood exactly what he had in mind. The notion that it was a phony never had occurred to him, and he could hardly hope to cash it by himself without delivering the goods. But if he was to be commissioned to negotiate for us, he had a perfect right to hold the stakes, of course.

I didn't think he had the least intention of negotiating. I certainly had no desire for him to try.

"If you can handle it, that's all there is to it," I said. "The company wants off the hook. They sent to Vera Cruz last fall to see how Max liked his tamales in the calaboose. He didn't seem to take an interest."

"That tea head!" he commented scornfully. He casually stuffed the check into his pocket and regarded me with something that came pretty close to only mildly dubious benevolence. "And where's the little lady coming into this?"

Suzy was making circles on the coffee table with the highball glass she hadn't touched before. She said demurely, "We were wondering if you might possibly misunderstand the purpose of this proposition, Mr. Henderson. Unless I came along."

The scalpel of sweet reason went in so efficiently he never felt a twinge of pain. It must have been that one, almost naive remark of hers that did the trick; he visibly relaxed and started concentrating on procedure rather than distrust. "Get Monty," he told Steve. "We're going for a ride."

"But Chief, it's gotta be a plant! I'm telling you the snooper's sure to put a finger on us for the johns...."

"Shaddup, I'm doing this for the insurance company. I got the proof of it right here." The very notion made him chortle with delight. "They're paying me a fee to snoop for them, y'understand? The johns ain't got a case on us that way at all."

The gray-faced man removed his shoulders from the wall, reluctantly, and wandered over to the desk to punch a buzzer button on the phone. "If it's that soft, you won't be needing me," he said, sarcastically to the point.

"Steve's got a date," I said. "She works at Paramount. She may be waiting for him now."

The gray-faced man gave me a bleakly diagnostic stare. Kicks Henderson broke out into another crash of laughter, nearly boisterous enough to spill him from his swivel chair. There was a knock behind us on the door, and Monty, who turned out to be a small wiry black man in khaki chauffeur's uniform, came striding in. He didn't quite salute or click his heels, but something in his walk said former army N.C.O. as unmistakably as if he were still wearing medals and chevrons. "Yeah, boss?"

Kicks managed to contain himself and scrambled ponderously to his feet. He capped the whiskey bottle, picked it up and threw it at the driver, who deftly fielded it and tucked it down under his arm. The five of us trooped out into the bar and up the basement stairs and on into the lobby through the noisy jungle of the bowling hall. The big man held the exit door for Suzy with a sweeping gesture, like an elephant according her precedence to the peanut stand. The driver marched off into the neon-glitter darkness of the parking lot. "Want us to follow you or wait for you?" I asked.

The big man slapped me on the back and practically knocked me through the front-porch floor. "You folks come right along with us. There's lots of room."

"There'll be more of it my way," I said.

A pair of airport-beacon headlights splashed into the driveway from the parking lot, and a marine-blue Lincoln Continental pulled up at the porch with Monty at the wheel. Its back seat door swung open to disclose pink quilted satinette upholstery.

I made a show of hesitating, holding Suzy back, and Steve closed in on us to ram a shoulder at my ribs. "Maybe you got a date yourself, huh, snooper?" he inquired.

"Okay, folks, all aboard!" Kicks brayed at us in his resounding train announcer's bellow. "Don't be bashful now, the heap's insured."

A Yellow cab swung in behind the Lincoln to disgorge four Knights of Araby in full regalia and leaning heavily into the breeze. They staggered past us arm in arm and disappeared into the Bristol Recreation Center, bawling "Mexicali Rose" in raucous harmony. Suzy was pulling at my sleeve and saying, "Darling, it's all right. We'll get there just as quickly, don't you see?"

I shrugged and helped her in. Kicks wedged between us, made the seat springs groan when he came down. Steve crowded after him and grabbed the strapontin confronting me before he slammed the door. The Lincoln slid away as if it ran on skis. It whipped around the turn at San Vicente and streaked west against the lights, too fast, but not quite fast enough to ask for trouble from the motor cop who ponderously straddled his machine across the intersection at the curb.

It was a cutie of a situation, and so far I was completely satisfied with it, the way a man is satisfied when he's made up his mind to walk into a tiger cage and finds the padlock off. The past half hour had proved extremely profitable and informative, I thought. Max Ulrich's confidence in his ability to produce the diamonds had been a valuable if somewhat ambiguous discovery, but then our present host had very pleasantly obliged us with the goods. The simple circumstance that Kicks knew where to look for baby meant a lot to me. It meant that now I knew myself, and from this fundamental knowledge could deduce a great deal more. I could deduce such things as how Max Ulrich had found out, and where my client was, and who had murdered Jeremiah Peter Bundy, and for what. I felt as smug about all those as if Globe-International had handed me a deerstalker, a meerschaum pipe and an enlarging glass, and told me to start looking keen into the camera. The only little item not quite taken care of yet was how we were supposed to stay alive for the next hour or two.

A briny tang had crept into the air that rushed in through the open window at my side. The Lincoln was already coasting down the palisades off Ocean Avenue and entering the steady stream of trailer trucks that rumbled north on Highway 101. Kicks Henderson was slumped against the sagging cushions, fast asleep and breathing slowly in a mighty diapason of a snore. I tapped his knee, and he came instantly awake to shy from me as if I'd used a knife instead of just a finger tip. "Where is this place we're headed for?" I asked.

He merely blinked and lounged back in his seat. "Okay, so it's a stash," I said impatiently. "Just stop the car a minute at a filling station, will you, please?"

"What for?"

"I want to use the washroom, is what for. You mind?"

This time it was the gray-faced man who chuckled, coarsely unamused. Kicks stirred uneasily and stared at me as if I'd made a social error of the first degree. "Hey, Monty, did you hear?"

The driver nodded placidly and tooled us smoothly off the highway, pulling up between the islands of the Chevron dealer at Paseo Miramar. I started to climb out, and Steve stuck out a leg to block the way. His handsome, sullen features bristled with suspicion. "Chief, I'm telling ya. . . ."

"Shaddup!" The big man's bark sounded embarrassed. "Let him go. You can go with him if you want. And watch the mouth, long as we got the little lady here!''

The rest rooms were disguised behind a tiny false-front Swiss chalet against the palisade, a walk of twenty yards. The gentlemen's department was immaculate and smelled of pine-oil-flavored germicide. Steve leaned against the wall's blue dollhouse tiles and crossed his arms. ''I like you, snooper,'' he informed me. ''You're a sweetheart, that's for sure. When this is over, me and you are gonna have a time, I promise ya.''

I pushed on past him, went into the cabinet and locked the door. A pedal ran the plumbing, and I stepped on that while scribbling furiously on a card and folding the result in a five-dollar bill. There was the customary switch above the flush box that would operate a signal in the station office, and a sign that said If Rest Room Needs Attention, Please Turn Up. I pressed it quietly home, released the pedal, slipped the folded bill under my wristwatch band and left the cabinet to make a show of washing hands. ''You're off the beam,'' I told the gray-faced man. ''There are a million ways we could've tipped the cops, but we can't use them kibitzing on this, not anymore than you. If they catch up with us and find that check on Kicks, they've got us cold on charges of compounding felony.''

He didn't drop his scowl, but it was hanging by a thread, and when he glanced into the cabinet he failed to notice the position of the switch. I held the rest-room door for him, and palmed the bill, and dumped it on the floor behind my hip when he walked out with me. It was close timing—one of the attendants was already coming from the office with a broom and pail, and giving us the beady eye as we passed by. The Lincoln took us back into its gaudy satin accolade and swept us out of there. It meshed into the highway traffic stream and changed its engine tune from dulcet whisper to sonorous drone. Kicks Henderson had drifted off to slumberland again; his weight felt like I had a grand piano in my lap. The flash reflection of a passing pair of headlights showed me Suzy's thoughtful smile across his bulging stomach paunch.

We hit the bypass curve this side of Malibu at something over ninety miles an hour.

The ocean disappeared, rejoined us for a stretch where road and shoreline were so closely wedded that the brightly phosphorescent surf seemed to be licking at the pavement's rim. At Zuma Beach we veered away from it once more, where clifflike headlands jutted off the mountains on our right to form a row of long and fairly shallow coves. The Lincoln's song of spinning tires on asphalt lost its steady treble pitch. A pair of painted gateposts sprang up in our headlights to announce the private thoroughfare that crossed the cliff. Monty caressed his brakes and sliced us through between these markers in a squealing hairpin turn.

Almost immediately the roadbed tilted steeply with the slope and roughened to a dirt-track corduroy. It quickly reached the crest and straightened out along the cliff's plateau before it curved toward the ocean through a windblown pine tree grove. A signboard at the second fork proclaimed The Lido Club—For Members Only on a bar fence crisscrossed with barbed wire. We swiveled clear of that and rolled into an open driveway circle, edged in jasmine shrubbery.

The house stood on the outpost border of the cliff. It was a large, two-storied Norman cottage with a mansard roof, sharply outlined in silhouette against the hazy moonlit sky. The Lincoln's blazing head-lights briefly sprayed its front of redwood logs and fieldstone panels and dark window panes before they swept around the turn and stopped under the narrow porte cochere. The motor died, the lights clicked off, and instantly the cricket chorus in the sagebrush swelled around us to a throbbing resonance that overruled the roaring of the surf.

Kicks Henderson woke up and vigorously blew his nose into a large bandanna handkerchief. "Okay, folks, everybody out!" he brayed.

"How'd you find out about this place?" I asked him artlessly.

He winked at me, as whimsically as an orangutan with a rose between its fangs. "Guys tell me things," he said. "This one moved out of here into a smaller layout, kind of suddenlike. I been consider-ing to drop around and see did he leave any junk behind."

I dutifully grinned for him. He was already herd-ing us toward the front door and away from the pro-tective shelter of the Lincoln's steel-clad flanks. The chilly ocean breeze came whistling past the house and carried in a stench of rotting kelp. The dial of my watch showed me 10:58.

There was a rusty squeak from the garage door on our left. The gray-faced man came strolling back, held up a finger to us. "Company," he mentioned carelessly.

Kicks frowned and punched a button on the front-door jamb. The mellow ding-dong of West-minster chimes responded from inside. I stepped on Suzy's toes and elbowed her against the wall.

A castanet of heels on parquet chattered briefly, and the door jarred back against its chain. Jane Lord stood in the crack, confronting Kicks behind a flush of irritation and embarrassment. She was in T-shirt and blue jeans and had a broad white ribbon in her hair; she looked as wholesome as a barrel of ripe apples, freshly harvested, and just about as hard to push around. "What do you want?"

He smirked at her. "You know me, miss?"

"I've seen you here before," she told him non-committally. "That doesn't mean you've got a right...." She glanced around him, saw me standing there and caught her breath. Bewildered recognition drained the angry flush, and took no notice of my warning scowl.

"What are you doing here?" she asked me, thoroughly perplexed.

11

SUZY SLIPPED PAST MY ELBOW, stepped into the light and said, "Don't worry, honey, we're the Marshalls. It's a little late, but Mr. Henderson has something very urgent on his mind. May we come in?"

There was a short and awkward pause, but she had brought it off. With those few words she had succeeded in creating the impression that I needed introduction, and that a refusal to admit us would amount to gross discourtesy. Jane Lord reluctantly removed the chain. "We were just leaving," she informed us pointedly.

The front door opened on a French-provincial living room that ran the full depth of the house. A massive fieldstone hearth adjoined the door and occupied the wall it served; three cedar logs were crackling merrily away in it and lent the room a rosy air of geniality in pleasant contrast to the murky winter night outside. The picture window at the other end gave us a dimly lighted patio that terminated in the double guardrail bordering the cliff. The boy McHugh, who had been lounging on the big divan under the window, scrambled to his feet when we came trooping in. His splendid athlete's body in a sweater and blue denim shorts rose like a tower almost to the ceiling beams.

Jane Lord flicked switches lighting up a table

lamp and two large wall brackets. She said uncertainly, "May I present my fiancé..." and stopped in open-mouthed dismay when Steve and Monty followed us into the room. The gray-faced man had slammed the door, and was now using it to give his back a rest. The wiry little black marched in and put the whiskey bottle he had been assigned to carry on the television console at the entrance to the dining room.

The boy McHugh looked stolidly surprised. He saw me standing by the mantelpiece but gave no sign of recognizing me. "Hey, Janie, what?"

She had retreated to his side and let him hold her hand. "That's what I'd like to know," she said indignantly.

Kicks Henderson stood facing them across the room. His size fourteens were planted wide apart; his monumental paunch, securely buttoned into that outrageous coat of bottle-green suede, was shaking with hilarity, as yet suppressed but obviously eager to explode. "Don't get excited, miss," he boomed. "Ain't nothing to it ought to bother you a bit. Expressman wouldn't bother you if he came by here to pick up a package, would he now?"

She made an effort to play up to him. "I don't suppose he would. Not if I'd been expecting him."

The belly laugh exploded, as per schedule. "Miss, if you'd expected me, there would of been no package for me to pick up."

"I'm sorry, but I just don't understand."

Kicks glanced over his shoulder, winked at me. "That's good, miss," he informed the girl. "We wouldn't want you to be wise to this. It wouldn't be so healthy for you if you was." He strolled toward the entrance to the dining room, which opened to his left.

She promptly stepped in front of him to block him, hands on hips. She had to look way up to meet his eyes; the gesture was preposterous but left her dignity completely unaffected. "Just a minute, please. Where are you going, may I ask?"

He could have walked right over her, if that had been his style. "Look, miss, your uncle done a little business with me sometimes."

"Maybe he did. I don't know anything about my uncle's business. If you believe he left something for you, you'll have to see his lawyers on Monday, Mr. What's-your-name-again. I certainly don't care for you to come on barging in here at this hour with all these friends of yours and prowl around. If you'll excuse me now, I think you'd better leave."

The boy McHugh had finally caught on. He moved a step or two in their direction, scowling with embarrassment. "You heard her, mister," he said sulkily. "We didn't ask you here."

Kicks did not even look at him. Steve sighed, removed his spinal column from the door and started taking off his tux again. This time he did not even trouble to roll up his sleeves or to unlimber his artillery. He crossed the room unhurriedly and pushed his hat back to inspect the boy, who towered head and shoulders over him. "Siddown, kid," he instructed him, almost good-naturedly.

Suzy was nudging me, and I glanced back at her and pursed my lips. It was another scene that didn't match the script, but this was not the time for me to call a story conference. I didn't think the picture would be likely to get too far out of sync while we were there. The boy was glowering at Steve in puzzled indecision. "Janie, honey..." he said doubtfully.

The gray-faced man crouched down and hit him

in the stomach, three quick blows, like a brisk workout on the heavy bag. Then he slid back one foot and dropped his shoulder, measured carefully and threw a punch the way a lumberjack would swing his ax. There was a solid, meaty thud when he connected, and the boy went reeling back until his wobbling legs were intercepted by the edge of the divan. He moved among the pillows for a while and suddenly lay still, both arms thrown wide, his wavy golden-yellow hair in helpless disarray. Jane Lord was on her knees beside him, quietly checking on his heartbeat, cradling him in her arms and delicately probing for a fracture in his clean-cut jaw. The gray-faced man stood over them and shook his head in mock astonishment. "Now ain't that something?" he submitted solemnly.

"Please go away." There was serene composure in her tone. "Bill's very strong—he could have killed you if he'd understood. He's never had to deal with anything like this before."

Steve smiled for her, a twisted smile of mixed derision and contempt. He put his coat back on, retreated to his post. Kicks Henderson had disappeared. I listened to his heavy footsteps cross the kitchen floor and drum on hardwood timber, going down the basement stairs. Suzy was pulling on my sleeve insistently. The crackling fireplace logs served to protect her urgent whisper. "Johnny, where's you-know-who?"

"He should've been here long ago!"

There was no question that she had a point, of course, although it had occurred to me that Max might easily have been held up. A hunted man can't always move as fast, or quite as openly, as we had moved ourselves. The fact remained that his delay

had thrown our timing out of gear, if timing was the
word for it, and if it had been possible for us at all to
do much more than hope and pray, and try to mud-
dle through somehow. The fact remained I wasn't
happy, having got this far. I didn't want to be in
that attractive, cozy living room, auditioning a
gaslight melodrama cast whose lines I could predict
only too well. I wanted to be chilly and uncomfort-
able, lying down behind a boulder on the beach outside where it was dark.

"Did you get word to Dave?"

I grinned at her and shrugged. The fireplace corner wasn't such a bad place after all. There were no
windows in that wall, and only two comparatively
small ones in the wall adjoining it. The picture window facing us across the room was probably its
weakest spot, although the narrow patio behind it
would be awkward to approach and would provide
less cover than a billiard table offers to a mouse.

Kicks Henderson was coming back. I heard him
climb the basement stairs, not half as quickly as
he had gone down. He used the big bandanna on
his face when he came stomping in at last, and
lowered himself gingerly into a handsome fan-back
chair that creaked in agonized protest under
his weight. Monty looked at him thoughtfully and
placed the whiskey bottle in his hand, uncapped.
Kicks rinsed his tonsils, fairly thoroughly, and
wiped his lips, and parked the open bottle in his
spacious lap. "Where is it, miss?" he peacefully inquired.

For all of twenty seconds there was nothing but
the crackling logs, the distant rumble of the surf. I
gave myself a cigarette; the spark wheel on my
lighter rasped as if it wanted to grow up and be a

rattlesnake. Jane Lord said frigidly, "Are you addressing me?"

"I ain't addressing you. I'm asking you."

"I see. What did you wish to know?"

"Look, miss, I want you shouldn't fuss with me.
I'm trying to remember you're supposed to be a
lady, even in them pants of yours."

She stared at him in stony silence. She was still on
her knees beside the divan, and the jeans, in that
position, did disparage her appearance to some
slight extent. The boy McHugh sat up and ran a
handful of uncertain fingers through his hair.
"What happened?" he demanded shakily.

She took his hand in both of hers and tightly clung
to it. "Hush, darling," she said quietly. "Not now."

The boy saw Kicks and Steve, remembered them
and swung his feet down to the floor. A crimson
flush of anger crept up from his sturdy neck to stain
the suntan bronze. "Are they still here?"

"They'll go away. They think we're hiding something that belongs to them."

Kicks had the bottle tilted back again. He was the
kind of drinking man who'd rather use a funnel
than a glass. This time he put it down beside him on
the floor, in something of a gesture of finality. "We
got all night," he mentioned placidly. "If I was you,
miss, I'd come clean before these fellows start to
take the joint apart."

The boy rose from the divan with Jane Lord still
clinging to him. He brought her up with him the
way he'd wear a watch charm on his wrist. He actually looked as if he could take on all five of us and
tie us up in little sailor knots, as pretty as you
please, before he'd even work himself into a
healthy sweat. "You guys get out of here," he

ordered us. "We don't want any trouble with you guys." It sounded childish, but it wasn't meant to be. I'd always had a slight suspicion Samson must have sounded childish, just before he started swinging with the jawbone of an ass.

The gray-faced man must have agreed with me. He didn't fool around with any striptease comedy this time. The Luger came into his hand, not in a quick and flashy draw but like a trusty tool deliberately chosen to perform a necessary job.

"Watch out, kid," he said mincingly. "This is a gun. It goes bang-bang, and you drop dead. So don't go getting any big ideas."

The boy McHugh ignored him, gently disengaged his captive hand and turned to Kicks, who promptly smashed the bottom of the whiskey bottle on the floor and showed him the remains. Jane Lord hysterically caught her breath and flung her arms around his waist. He started dragging her, and Steve brought up the Luger, aimed it coolly at his heart. Suzy grabbed my sleeve, and I said sharply, "Just a minute, Bill!"

He hesitated, turned his classically sculptured profile half in my direction. "Listen, let me ask you something," I suggested. "Did you know that poison ivy won't affect the skin of Eskimos and babies under fourteen months of age?"

Kicks Henderson's explosive guffaw shook the roof. Even the wiry little black contributed a grin. The gray-faced man lowered his gun and scowled at me. The boy was staring at me in complete confusion. "What's that got to do with it?"

"That's what I'm trying to explain."

Jane Lord was pulling him toward the couch. "Please, darling, let's sit down and listen to the man," she urged. The glance she flashed in my direction brought me twenty years' supply of puzzled gratitude. I leaned an elbow on the mantelpiece and blew a smoke ring, and got set to make my second-best after-dinner speech and gain a little time.

The front door's silver-toned Westminster chimes rang mellowly to intervene.

Too many things started to happen, much too fast. I ducked and tackled Suzy's legs and brought her down with me to hit the rug. The Luger filled the room with crashing sound; the picture window broke and jangled in a hundred fragments on the patio tiles. Somewhere outside at least two other guns were working, and the slugs were banging on the walls in fitful hammer blows. The driver, Monty, knocked the table lamp away and pitched a chair into the wall brackets, killing the lights. Kicks Henderson was in the kitchen, shouting orders in a bull-like roar.

It was a clumsy sneak attack, and it had failed; there was no doubt of that. The doorbell chimes had been intended to distract us while they took us from the rear. The gray-faced man had not been fooled; the Luger's quick barrage had swept the patio clear. Now he was out there, crunching through the broken glass and taking pot shots at them from the corner of the house, while Monty charged out through the front door to the car and Kicks was firing through the kitchen windows, covering his move. I got my feet back under me and helped the little woman up. The rosy flicker from the fireplace logs revealed our host and hostess, huddled close together on the couch. They seemed to have been shocked into a daze, but otherwise appeared unharmed.

The firing stopped, and Monty darted back into the room. He slammed the front door, threw the chain on it and dumped a stack of ammunition boxes on the floor. Kicks Henderson came waddling from the dining room; the Army .45 in his big hairy paw looked like a trinket from the five-and-dime. He glanced at the supply of groceries for it, a trifle doubtfully. "You folks'd better take these kids upstairs," he boomed at us. "This ain't your shindig, and the little lady could get hurt."

"Who are your friends?" I asked him artlessly.

His snort was coarsely eloquent. "That tea head. Figuring I shopped him to the spicks, after he got me on the phone from Vera Cruz last year, the chump. We'll fix him right this time."

"You didn't quite explain that when you took my check," I said. "This was supposed to be a deal."

"That so? You said for me to handle it. You paid your geetus and you'll get your deal. Just leave it lay there for a minute, will ya, pal?"

Steve vaulted lightly back in through the picture window from the patio and crossed the room to elbow me aside. He fed the Luger, crammed the pockets of his tux with cartridges. "Where's Little Phoebe?" he demanded almost cheerfully.

"They found her, boss," said Monty with a grimace. "They done cased the trunk. Shuah lucky Ah kept this heah belly medicine under the seat."

Steve whistled meditatively and cocked an ear. "I don't hear anything," he said. "Not yet, that is."

Suzy, herding Jane Lord and Bill McHugh into the dining room and up the winding maple staircase to the second floor, glanced back at me and waved. I wandered after them and caught them on the landing, steering them into the guest room over the garage. It was a large and pleasant bedroom, done in knotty pine with rustic furniture, including twin four-posters neatly made and covered with white monk's-cloth spreads. A hazy yellow moon was reflected in the dresser mirror and revealed the sullenly resigned expression on the faces of our charges. "Get this straight now, both of you," I said. "You're in a nasty bind, and so are we. But we can maybe see you through, if you play ball with us. You two stay put right here—don't show a light, don't smoke and don't go near the windows. That's just about all there is to it."

"You lied to us this morning," said the girl resentfully. "How do we know if we can trust you now?"

Somewhere outside six shots went off in quick succession, and the Luger's vicious whipcrack snapped in tart reply. Glass tinkled gaily in the living room. I said, "You may or may not realize it, but your uncle was a fence, Miss Lord. It follows that you must expect insurance dicks to lie to you."

She jerked away from me as if I'd called her names, and flung herself facedown upon the nearest bed. She wept almost without a sound, but she was clutching at the pillows with a grip of fierce despondency. The boy stood over her and watched her helplessly. Suzy had found a phone extension on the night stand and was jiggling the receiver bar. "They've cut the wires," she told me brightly.

"Maybe we should sue them, honey doll," I said, and pulled her out with me into the corridor. "Listen, you stick around and keep an eye on things. I'd better circulate a bit and see what's going on."

She quickly kissed me on the mouth. "It's awful, darling, isn't it? Will Dave get up here soon?"

"I doubt it very much."

"You mean you didn't . . ." she began, and bit her pretty lips to watch me from across the banister while I ran down the winding stairs.

The situation was a little tricky, but by no means desperate. The house was sturdily constructed, not too large and favorably placed. Three well-armed and determined men could reasonably hope to hold their own in there against four times their number, if the latter did not come equipped with tear gas, hand grenades or heavy armament. The south wall, which accommodated the garage, was bare of first-floor window space. Monty the driver crouched behind the kitchen window, covering the front, which offered him an open field of fire across the driveway circle, broken only by the narrow archway of the porte cochere. The two small windows in the north wall of the living room commanded twenty rods of open lawn, and Steve was on his knees between them, sighting down his pistol barrel through a crack in the Venetian blinds. This left the the patio gallery, the cliff side and the broken picture window, easily defended from the divan couch. Kicks Henderson reclined among the cushions, comfortably settled down behind the heavy-cannon muzzle of his Army Colt.

He heard me on the stairs and glanced over his shoulder, fretfully. "Hey, you ain't leaving us?" he asked me. "Don'tcha like the service, pal?"

"Just shopping," I assured him, ducking through the open kitchen door. The driver grinned for me and suddenly popped up to pump three rapid shots at something moving in the shrubbery along the driveway to his right.

A single slug came back in answer, smacked into

the plaster with a hollow thump, two feet behind my ears. I swore, and slithered down the basement stairs considerably faster than decorum would prescribe. I couldn't figure out the tactics of the other side. They probably had planned to take their time. They could afford it, too—we were at least two miles from the big coastal highway, while the nearest house might be a thousand yards away, and would most likely be unoccupied this chilly January night.

The basement lights had been left on. The basement was a nice big playroom, burrowed deep into the cliff and finished in white-glazed cement with a maroon-and-lime-green-checkered composition floor. It had a regulation Ping-Pong table and a built-in bamboo bar, a rack of fishing rods and gear, two large stuffed bass in driftwood frames. Even the ashtrays were a set of burnished abalone shells. A ventilator shaft gave passage to the rumble of the breakers and the briny pungency of the ocean through its insect screen. The only minor disconformity in there consisted of a rather handsome six-point blacktail deer head, mounted on the wall over the bar.

The furnace was a modern Honeywell, and sat with its hot-water tank in the southeastern corner, close against the walls. I listened to its gentle drone; upstairs, the broken windows would be working on its thermostat. There was an old and fairly seedy plumber's friend leaning against the water tank. It was the only tool in sight, and I had trouble thinking of a reason for its presence in that spot. I picked it up and looked at it and put it back again in casual experiment. Its suction cup stuck to the floor, and when I pulled the handle something moved a little

under it. I grunted, kicked it loose and tried again.
A section of the floor came up, about ten inches
square and backed with half an inch of lead to hold
it down. It fitted snugly with a hairline seam to
match the gaudy checker pattern, and it offered access to a tiny strongbox cover with a combination
lock.

The lid came open easily enough; Kicks had not
even bothered to spin back the dial of the lock. The
box was lined with dark-blue velvet trays. They
were as empty as a politician's promises on Inde-
pendence Day.

I shrugged it off, restored the floorboard section
to its status quo, and had one foot already on the
stairs when it occurred to me that deer-head
trophies are not usually taken with a fishing rod.

The painted wooden locker on the wall behind
the Ping-Pong table had not caught my interest
before. I took a walk that way, not fast, not slow,
and tried the door. It asked me for a key, or for a
good stiff kick under its padlock hinge. I didn't
have a key, but I was wearing brand-new rubber
heels.

There was a single shelf stacked with a bunch of
camping gadgets, hunting knives and outdoor junk.
There were three guns in canvas hoods: a target .22,
a sporting rifle and a twelve-gauge shotgun, all in
excellent condition, beautifully cleaned and
greased. I started humming "Yankee Doodle" in a
fine, sonorous baritone, and wrapped the rifle and
the shotgun in a section of last Sunday's *Post-
Courier*, and stuffed my pockets with four clips of
.30-30's and a dozen shells.

The driver did not even glance at me when I
passed through the kitchen with my package, but

Kicks Henderson looked up from the divan. "What's that you got?"

"They had a rummage sale down at the hardware store," I said, and kept on walking, made the bottom of the winding stairs and started up. He glowered after me and slowly shifted weight to bring the Colt around. From somewhere out in front arrived a sudden racket like a fleet of trucks with badly timed ignition systems racing down the hill. The front door sprang a score of leaks and violently banged against its chain. Both Steve and Monty opened fire. The blitz was on, and Little Phoebe had come home to roost.

I gained the stairway landing in three jumps, and Suzy almost knocked me over, racing down the corridor from the big master bedroom at the other end. She hugged my arm that grabbed the banister; her voice was dancing with excitement. "Look at what I found!"

It was too dark to see, but what she made me touch appeared to be a small revolver, probably a Banker's Special .32. I probed its chambers with a finger tip and pressed the butt into her hand. "That's fine," I said. "You better leave the hammer down for now. Don't hesitate to use it if we get into a pinch."

"They kept it in a dresser drawer," she informed me. "Don't you want it? Johnny, what's that frightful noise outside?"

I was already hustling for the master bedroom and uncovering my arsenal. "It seems the boys downstairs were carrying around a chopper in their car, and Max got hold of it," I said. "We can't use any part of that—it gives the other side a little bit too much the best of it. I'll have to see what I can do to smooth the wrinkles out."

The master bedroom had another picture window overlooking the Pacific, but its general appointments were surprisingly severe and masculine: bare plaster, oak-beam ceiling, corded homespun rugs, a set of plain Grand Rapids furniture most wealthy men would hardly trouble storing in the loft. I dumped the shotgun on the bed and slammed a clip into the rifle's magazine. There were two narrow casements in the front wall, both affording me a moonlight panorama of the driveway circle with its fallow flower beds and parched Bermuda lawn. I raised the sash in one of them, and cautiously pushed the rifle barrel through the screen.

The grease gun was behind a pine tree in the grove that swallowed up the road beyond the lawn, some sixty yards away and comfortably out of pistol range. It fired in measured bursts, methodically chopping at the kitchen and the living room, and showed staccato flashes briefly blending, like a tiny yellow flower in the woods. If it remained there, unmolested, it would almost certainly accomplish something—either killing the defenders or preoccupying their attention to a point where an attack by storm might very well come off.

Suzy was breathing down my neck and watching me expectantly. I snicked the rifle's bolt and checked its sights; it was an old converted Springfield that would just as likely throw too high and possibly three feet to either side. "You want to get your head blown off, petunia?"

She hurriedly drew back. "What about you? Are you supposed to be the Iron Man?"

"They showed me how to do this for a living," I reminded her, and squatted down to take a sight. The submachine gun promptly stuttered to a halt;

the woods were dark again, and quiet but for the cricket chorus in the brush. A single set of headlights topped the rise behind the Lido Club and blazed up through the trees. The distant engine mutter rapidly increased in pitch and volume till the car came rushing down the driveway to pull up behind the Lincoln in the porte cochere. It was an open Jaguar coupe; the driver, wrapped in camel's hair and in a white silk scarf, serenely started to take off his gloves, as if he planned to have a drink with us and stay awhile.

I left the Springfield dangling in the window screen and raced out of the bedroom, through the corridor and down the stairs. Steve was already at the door, and had obligingly removed the chain and flattened himself back against the fireplace wall. His gun, as steady as a vulture's beak at mealtime, pointed at the crack behind the busted lock. "Hold it!" I snapped at him. "The press has just arrived!"

Mr. Alfonso Baron failed to note the ragged maze of bullet holes that graced the door. He knocked on it, politely, felt it give under his touch, and stepped into the room. His sharp long nose was wrinkled, trying to identify the acrid stench of cordite fumes; his eyes were blinking in an effort to accommodate themselves. He saw me only when I reached him, seized his arm and hastily jerked him aside. "Ah, Marshall, there you are! I got your message, and I came out right away.... What seems to be the trouble here?"

The submachine gun in the pine trees made a noise like a pneumatic drill, dispatching half a dozen slugs in through the open door.

12

THE GRAY-FACED MAN said raucously, "So you got wise and left a message, did ya, snooper, huh?"

The Luger's eager muzzle jammed into my kidneys, prodding me into the relative security of the dining room. Mr. Alfonso Baron clutched the stairway colonnade; his knees were shaking visibly, and his suavely vicious features were a sallow mask of terror. *"Snooper!"* he was shrilling. "But. . .but I don't *understand*! Who are you men? Why did you send for me?"

"Shaddup!"

Kicks Henderson, on the divan, looked like the very wrath of God. A flying splinter had cut up one jowl, and blood was seeping in the furrow of his double chin. Gunsmoke and grease had smeared ferocity on him like war paint, and his bulging bulldog eyes were hard as ten-cent marbles, and a little mad. "You say this guy is a reporter?" he inquired.

"He publishes the *Movieland Observer*," I informed him with a shrug.

"That rag," said Kicks. He interposed an adjective that jarred its beneficiary like a blow. "You get him up here like he says?"

"What if I did?"

"How did you know about this place?" he roared at me.

"I had another client, who had mentioned it to me," I said. "It's a long story, Mr. Henderson. I doubt if you'd have time and patience to appreciate my telling it just now."

The driver, in the kitchen, opened fire again. The grease gun countered with another burst that rattled off the cars outside. The gray-faced man said, "Chief, I warned ya, didn't I? He must of fingered us for Max while he was at it, can'tcha see that now?"

"You're off the beam again, Steve," I protested, fairly speciously.

"Shaddup," said Kicks. The stony bulldog eyes were down to slits. He jerked a thumb over his shoulder at the open front door. "Out!" he ordered. "Both of 'em!"

The Luger prodded me again and swept around to Baron, who released the colonnade, sank to his knees and lost his dinner on the floor. From halfway down the stairway, Suzy spoke up crisply. "As you were, boys," she instructed us. "Back to your jobs, and I mean quick, before this thing goes off!" The shotgun I'd left on the bed was cradled in her arms, its double hose-pipe barrels yawning at us all impartially.

Steve hesitated, and I edged away from him to make him feel alone. The fat man on the divan found a chuckle somewhere, and succeeded thereby in increasing my respect for him. "You heard the little lady," he directed imperturbably.

"But Chief...."

I grabbed Alfonso Baron's collar, yanked him to his feet and started marching him upstairs. He almost fainted, brushing past the shotgun; I was forced to prop him up and boost him to the landing, where he tumbled on the parquet in a sprawl. "Your pants are wet, sweet Antoinette," I said. "This isn't quite the piece of cake you wanted, is it, chum?"

Suzy came up beside me, frowning in provoked disfavor. "Darling, what possessed you, dragging him into this business?"

I took the empty shotgun from her hands and broke it open, reached into my pocket for a couple of shells. "Nice teamwork, sugar bun," I said.

"You didn't mean to get him killed?"

"I meant to demonstrate to him that even blackmail doesn't always pay," I said, and slipped a shell into both barrels, clicked the safety on and tucked the shotgun back under her arm. "Of course I hadn't figured on us being on the inside of this mousetrap deal. I guess that gag of mine about let's you and him fight wasn't such a brilliant notion after all."

Alfonso Baron moaned for us, rolled over on the runner carpet and was sick again. I kicked him in the ribs, not very hard. "Get up, chum, you're just blocking traffic here."

Jane Lord said from the guest-room doorway, "Can I help? Did he get hurt?" She sounded cool and altogether self-possessed once more. The boy McHugh, looming behind her in the shadows, reached an arm around her waist protectively. She gently disengaged herself and knelt at Baron's side to strike a match and lift his eyelids.

"He's in shock," she told us soberly.

"He wasn't hit," I said. "But help yourself. Just take him out of here so we won't stumble over him."

She rose and gave a nod to Bill, who stooped to

grasp a handful of the camel's hair and lifted Baron in it like a sack of groceries. He carried him into the guest room, dropped him on the nearest bed. Outside, the submachine gun rattled off another burst. "Those lads are getting out of hand," I said, and ran back to the master bedroom, down the corridor. The Springfield was still on the window ledge, its barrel poked out through the screen. I crouched behind it, got the little yellow flower in my sights and squeezed the trigger, carefully, as if it might break off.

The Springfield coughed; the little yellow finger disappeared. Almost immediately it flashed up again, and plaster, broken glass and chunks of wood rained down on me where I had flopped under the ledge. One slug came whistling past me like a mockingbird; another banged on metal and went ricocheting around the room as if it wanted out. Suzy peeked in on me from behind the bathroom door. "You missed him," she enlightened me.

"Well, I'll be switched," I said. "Is that a fact?"

"If you're about to try again, you'd better use this window, laughing boy," she mentioned frigidly. "The panelwork looks much more solid here."

I ripped the rifle from the screen and ducked into the bathroom; Little Phoebe was already back to chopping at the living room. The bathroom was a pleasant place to be, with lots of heavy chromium and porcelain, and slabs of real marble on the walls. It had a shower stall and the usual conveniences, but the only casement was a pretty small affair, high up above the tub. "What do you think this is, Jack and the beanstalk?" I protested.

"You can make it, darling. From the pipes."

She had me with my insteps anchored in the

plumbing and inclining at a crazy angle to the ledge. It could be done, but it was only slightly less precarious than hanging from the curtain rollers by my teeth. "Here comes another item for these bathroom accident statistics," I suggested cheerfully.

This time I drew a bead, allowing for about a yard's worth elevation in trajectory. The Springfield's kick upset my balance, nearly spilling me into the tub. The noisy little yellow flower blinked and faded out. I slammed another cartridge home and braced myself, but it did not come back on tap. Even the cricket chorus faltered in surprise. "I think we may have slowed him down a bit," I said.

Jane Lord knocked on the bathroom door and walked in from the corridor. She eyed my fancy acrobatics on the plumbing fixtures without interest. "One of your friends downstairs seems to be injured," she advised us. "Do you want me to look after him?"

I managed to dismount without unreasonable damage to my dignity. "They're not exactly friends of ours," I said. "But we won't stop you if you'd like to play the lady with the lamp. I'll go down with you, if you feel uneasy with those fellows."

She was in the bathroom closet digging out a first-aid kit. "I'll be all right," she promised. "Thank you very much. Bill can take care of me."

Suzy was sitting on the laundry basket with the shotgun on her lap. Her pretty white cotton was streaked with grease, and her new hairdo had been generously sprayed with plaster dust, but she would probably have had Great-Grandma Willet's renegade Comanches on the run by now. I grinned at her and told her to stay put. I caught my own reflection in the mirror, winced at it, and wandered out after the Lord girl, with the rifle trailing by its sling.

The turkey shoot had been suspended, but there was considerable heated conversation in the living room. I listened to it from the landing—they were arguing about how bad it was, and what ought to be done with it. At last the boy McHugh appeared, carrying Steve across the dining room and up the winding staircase, holding him as if he were a baby in his arms. The gray-faced man hung limp; his dress shirt was a sticky mess of bright red blood. But he was fully conscious, and he actually squeezed a smirk out of his tight-lipped mouth.

"Some fun, huh, kid?" he asked the boy, who scowled at him embarrassedly and laid him gently on the guest room's second bed. I walked in after them, out of the shadows on the landing, and Steve saw the rifle I was trailing. "So you pulled the plug on them."

"A little late," I said. "And maybe not for very long. You caught a packet, soldier, didn't you?"

Jane Lord brushed past me with a pair of bandage scissors and began to cut his shirt away. "He needs a doctor," she advised me, solemnly professional.

Alfonso Baron, on the other bed, released a stricken moan, and tossed himself around under the blankets she'd put over him. "We may need half a dozen doctors pretty soon," I said. "We need a task force of Marines right now." The Luger's butt protruded from a pocket of Steve's dinner jacket, and I slipped it out and stuck it in my belt. I'd gathered almost half of all the ordnance that had been brought into action, but it wasn't doing me much good. I knew I didn't have a prayer to keep this show under control.

Steve looked romantic in the moonlight, with a wad of cotton gauze taped to his rugged fighter's chest and slowly seeping claret, but the girl glanced up at me and shook her head. I lighted a cigarette and offered it to him; he puffed on it contentedly, although his flat-voiced snarl had been reduced to little better than a whisper. "Whyn'tcha go on down'n' give the chief a hand? You got us into this."

"What makes you think I'm on your side?" I asked him. "Do the best you can for him," I told the girl, and lugged my load of slightly used exterminator gear into the corridor again.

Suzy was at the bathroom mirror, trying to effect repairs. She'd wrapped herself into a wrinkled terry robe and turned the portable electric heater on. The basement furnace could not seem to cope with all those open doors and broken windows, and a California winter night can drop you all the way from 90 degrees down to 35 degrees. She paused with lipstick in midair. "What's happening?"

"Looks like two down and four to go," I said. "The boys outside are probably regrouping, as we used to put it in the Army, but they've got it made, unless we throw in with the local team. The place can't be defended by two guns, and it's too isolated for this clambake to invite official curiosity."

"I don't suppose there's any way we can get out of here," she speculated carefully.

"Well, yeah, there is. They've got a ventilator in the cellar big enough to wriggle through. Kicks couldn't make it, but we could. The trouble is you'd hit the cliffside, eighty feet or so above the beach. Without a rope it'd be pretty risky stuff."

"And it might take an hour before we'd find a

phone or get up to the highway," she reflected. "Johnny, we can't leave those kids that long, or even Mr. Baron. There's no telling what that mob outside will do to them if they break in."

I'd stuck my nose into the master bedroom for a checkup on the scenery and caught a whiff of a familiar, rather heady stench that suddenly suggested certain possibilities. The little woman said behind me, "Such a shame it is, at that, because we've got our hands on what we wanted here, and we could just take off with it."

"How's that again?"

She smiled for me demurely in the mirror, pointing at the laundry basket with her lipstick. I stared at her, lifted the lid and moved a bunch of dirty towels to uncover what at first inspection in the hazy moonlight looked exactly like a pack rat's nest: odd scraps of metal, strings of colored beads, a wad of tissue paper and a small black wallet. "Whooie! What made you frisk this thing, petunia?"

"I didn't," she explained. "I put it there. Johnny, I was just cold, and I'd already found a big raffia bag of beach clothes in the shower stall, so I pulled out this robe, and all that junk was wrapped in it."

Outside, the submachine gun opened up for business again. I used a naughty word and dropped the Springfield on the water tank of the commode. "We'll have to try and flag the rescue squad," I said. "This may not even work, and it's an awful chance to take, but I'm afraid we've got to take it, sugar bun. You'd better quit your primping and duck out of here."

"What did you have in mind?" she questioned

me. "Darling, that wallet—it's the one we're hunting, isn't it?"

I was already cramming it into her shoulder bag, and pouring in the rest of what she'd found. There was no doubt that it was filled with an assortment of what goes into the better type of wedding rings, and that the other stuff would run the bundle to a couple of million dollars, but I had no time to play with it just then, so I took Suzy's arm and shoved her out into the corridor and slammed the door on her. I seized the bathroom heater by its insulated handle, yanked the cord and dragged the heater with its elements still glowing cherry red into the bedroom, kicked the screen out of the nearest window, flung the heater out and threw myself flat on my face.

The blast of the explosion wasn't quite as loud as I'd expected, but the flames shot up above the window to the roof in a magnificent and searing pyrotechnical display. The porte cochere collapsed into a crashing turbulence of shattered brick and masonry. The bullet-riddled gas tanks of two cars will commonly oblige with something of a spectacle, if thoughtfully provided with a light.

Behind the shrubbery around the driveway, Little Phoebe stammered to a halt, then started chopping at the living room again. They'd moved her from the pine-tree grove and probably found cover for her closer in, among the cliffside rocks, where she could rake the vulnerable north wall that adjoined the patio. I crawled into the corridor and shut the bedroom door to stop the draft that was already sucking sparks into the house. Jane Lord stood on the landing, and behind her there were sounds of scuffling, and Alfonso Baron's howls of panic.

"Keep him in there, please, and close the door," I said. "There isn't any danger yet. I'll warn you if the fire gets out of hand."

She nodded and complied. Suzy had grabbed my sleeve and handed me the shotgun. "Wasn't that a lovely noise!" she praised me eagerly.

"Yeah, this is living," I agreed and listened to the roaring of the flames out front. They'd die out soon enough, unless the roof caught fire, in which event we'd have to run for it. "Maybe you'd rather be a farmer, after all, petunia," I said.

Suzy clung to my arm. She'd taken off the terry robe, and she was shivering a little. "Johnny, who killed Mr. Bundy?"

"Don't you know?"

"I think so. But I don't see _how_...."

"That part of it is not our job," I pointed out to her. "And even if it were, there's nothing we can do about it now."

Downstairs Kicks Henderson was firing at the corner of the patio. The driver, Monty, in the kitchen had been silent for some time, but suddenly there came three rapid shots from that direction, and the rattle-thud of something heavy banging into furniture and on the floor. I disengaged myself, pushed Suzy back, and moved up to the staircase landing on my rubber heels. Across the banister I could see Mickey Kroll emerging from the kitchen, walking just as quietly out into the dining room. He glanced up at the stairs but failed to see me lurking in the shadows; in his hand, the stubby little .38 appeared almost inconsequentially innocent. The moonlight caught his pimply satyr sneer; he'd lost the porkpie skimmer, and he was a ragged scarecrow covered with wet sand and dust. They'd found the ventilator shaft, and he'd come up the cliff somehow, removed the screen and crept into the basement, taking Monty from the rear.

There was no reasonable way I could have stopped him once he'd got that far. The shotgun would not bear on him from where I stood. It was a very handsome Belgian piece they wouldn't sell you at the store for less than six or seven hundred dollars, but it wasn't built to shoot around a corner, or into the crazy angles of those winding stairs. Steve's Luger might have served the purpose, but I hadn't had a chance to check its load, and Mickey wasn't going to hold still for me while I was shifting guns around and making noises like a bunch of cops.

I couldn't see the living room from this far up, but it was not particularly hard to form a picture of what was about to happen, and of what would follow afterward. I had about five seconds left to make a hellishly embarrassing decision while the ice cubes in my stomach rattled like a set of poker dice. The submachine gun stopped, and Mickey moved out of my view. His shrill, sarcastic high-school-boy-gone-haywire voice said nastily, "That does it, Jack. Sit up'n'beg, there's a good dog."

Kicks must have dropped the Colt on the divan—I didn't hear it fall. I put one foot out on the stairs, the way you test the water in your swimming pool on a cool morning in the early spring, and let it take my weight, not very fast. The staircase didn't creak, or anyway not loud enough to overcome the steady crepitation of the burning cars outside in front. There was a quick tattoo of running footsteps on the patio gallery. Max Ulrich's nasal diction sounded even more fastidious than I remembered

from the Club Tahiti, "So you figured you could
pack us in!"

"So what?" The big man's booming rumble hit
the ceiling rafters and bounced back at him. "Tea
head!" he shouted scornfully, and burst into his
irrepressible, outrageously noisy guffaw of a laugh.

By then I'd climbed down far enough. The archway to the living room was visible, and Mickey in it
with his back to me. Max stood on the divan, with
Little Phoebe cradled in his arms. The flames outside reflected in his horn-rimmed spectacles and
lent his bland accountant's features a demoniac
malignancy no dope fiend's nightmare could have
matched. Kicks Henderson was facing them, his fat
behind against the north wall and his huge red paws
linked on his head. For all he knew, he didn't have
another breath left in his body, but he used the one
he could still count on for that crashing, monstrous
laugh of his. I clicked the safety off the shotgun,
dug my heels in, hooked one arm around the banister and said, "Okay, gents, pick'em up! This is
where you get off the bus. . . ."

Bat Wiley saw me first. He had been leaning on
the broken picture-window frame, a pistol dangling
from his left hand, while his right arm was stuck in
his belt, the sleeve torn off, most of his shirt
wrapped over it and leaking blood. He grunted in
surprise and darted off along the patio gallery
before the shotgun swung around to him. Max
Ulrich froze on the divan, still with his back to me,
but Mickey Kroll had whirled. The stubby .38 was
pointing at me from his hip; the big bravado sneer
was on his pimply face and twitching his impossible
goatee. "You better drop it, youngster, quick!" I
warned him urgently.

He made a vulgar and impractical suggestion, gave me his falsetto chuckle, threw a slug at me. It takes an expert shot to hit a man at twenty feet in that position, but he came too close, and it was certainly no time to let him try again. I fired one barrel at his legs, but it was open choke, and at that distance it struck high; he floundered on the carpet for a while before he could lie still. Max Ulrich glanced over his shoulder, saw the second barrel staring at his head and carefully put down the sub-machine gun on the couch before he raised his hands.

Kicks Henderson was reaching for it when I snapped at him. He hastily drew back, provoked with me. "Hey, listen, pal, that thing is dangerous. Ya wanna run the book and own the horses, too?"

There was a shot outside, immediately followed by a whole barrage. Behind me on the staircase, Suzy gave a tiny whimper of dismay. She had the little Banker's Special, and she'd probably been at my elbow all the time. "That man who got away.... Do we have to go through all that again?"

"Sounds more like the Marines have landed, candy face," I said.

She brushed on past me and went hurrying across the dining room to Mickey's body, sprawling on the rug. "Don't touch him." I said quietly, "There's nothing you can do for him."

She flinched from what she saw, and dropped the Banker's Special on a chair. More footsteps crunched across the patio. A shout came from the lawn, "Put on your lights in there!"

I broke the shotgun, walked downstairs and laid it on the table, snapped the switches in the dining room. The house filled up with men who brandished guns and handcuffs, men who whistled at the damage—strange men and familiar-looking men and men in white who carried stretchers, men in helmets lugging chemical extinguishers upstairs.

The man who prompted me aside into a corner was still wearing a dark purple turban, and I'd seen him last when he was on the front porch of the Bristol Recreation Center bawling "Mexicali Rose."

"I'm Anderson, Postal Inspector," he informed me in a Texas drawl. "You folks been throwin' quite a party for yo'selves."

"I'm Marshall, taxpayer," I said. "Mind telling me what happened to deprive us of your company so long?"

He grinned for me, not too self-consciously. "Our driver lost you on the highway," he explained. "We were explorin' every sideroad between Malibu and Oxnard when we caught the fireworks y'all were sendin' up."

It was the filling-station stop we'd made that would have thrown them off, of course. They were the team from San Antonio who had flown in that afternoon, and they'd depended on the local talent for assistance.

"Who's your driver?" I inquired.

He pointed with his chin; I recognized the heavy-set young sheriff's deputy from Hogan's office and suppressed a smile. Alfonso Baron tottered down the stairs all by himself, and shied away from me to stumble out into the night. Suzy came up to us, was introduced to Anderson, and proudly started to unload her shoulder bag. The Texan caught his head between his hands in humorous despair. "You folks'll have to spend the next five years in coh't," he sympathized with us.

"But not to sue for the rewards," I said, and wandered off to buttonhole the heavy-set young man. "You looking for me, Sheriff?"

He woke up and recognized me. "Yes, sir, the Lieutenant wants to see you right away. We had a message from him on the radio, just when we saw the fire."

I edged him over to where Kicks was leaning gloomily against the mantelpiece and staring at the nippers on his wrist. "Is the Lieutenant in his office?"

"No, sir, he's at Shady Dell. There's a patrol car here from Malibu; I'll ask the boys if you can ride with them."

I reached behind me, found the pocket in which Kicks had stuffed my check, extracted same and palmed it neatly up my sleeve. The fat man growled at me in startled indignation, but I was already piloting the deputy away. "You'd better come upstairs with me," I told him confidentially. "We've kept two people there on ice for the Lieutenant, and they're likely to object if I invite them on this trip."

He dug a five-cent notebook out, leafed through it and consulted with a hasty pencil scribble. "Miss Jane Lord and Mr. William R. McHugh," he said. "Yes, sir, I know. Lieutenant Hogan's message said I was to bring them in."

13

THE ROOM WAS TILED in oyster white clear to the ceiling line, and smelled unpleasantly of formalin. It had a few straight-backed white plastic chairs, two glass-front closets filled with instruments and bottled chemicals, a lab bench built against one wall, and two large oblong slabs of marble in the center mounted on twin pedestals of stainless steel. The light in there was harsh enough to curl your hair. It came from fluorescent banks of the industrial variety, suspended in reflector domes above the empty slabs and bench.

Lieutenant David Hogan, Confidential Squad, sat in the window bay that overlooked the swan lake, talking with a chubby little man who wore a full black spade beard and a beautifully tailored suit of double-breasted tweeds. The mortuary manager was standing by and frowning at the conversation, like my Uncle Ralph would frown at us when we disputed his contention about Cincinnatus having been the greatest general who ever lived. A lanky gray-haired sergeant-deputy from Homicide whose name was Kennedy and whom I'd come across before, stood at the other window, smoking a cigar and staring glumly at the lake.

It was a little after two o'clock on Sunday morning when we walked into this cheerful spot. Joe

Kennedy ignored us, and the mortuary manager just glanced at us reproachfully. The bearded little man looked up and showed a merry twinkle in his eye. Hogan inspected us through shaggy brows without a flicker of expression on his corrugated-leather face. "You kids should ought to take a bath and get a change of clothes," he said. "The way I hear, you made out pretty good."

From him, this was effusive praise indeed. Suzy said dulcetly, "Why, Dave, you're positively generous this lovely morning. Is there something we can do for you to show our gratitude?"

"I got to take a statement from you kids, is all." He saw me looking at the empty slabs and added, "Yeah, we dug him up and put him back again."

"Well, then you know," I said. "We thought you'd want to check the deal. What killed him, Doc?" I asked the bearded little man, who was the county coroner's pathologist.

He had a sunnily good-humored chuckle for me. "Pulmonary embolism," he informed us with a wink, and tapped his handsome, painted silk foulard, as if he wanted to make sure we'd understand just where that was.

I stared at him and shrugged; Suzy had caught her breath. "Oh, fine," I said. "If that's the way it is, you won't need any statements from us, Dave. We might as well go home."

"So what's the rush?" demanded Hogan. "Stick around until we've had some powwow with the family." He glanced at Kennedy, who nodded and strolled out into the little anteroom connecting with the hall.

When he returned, Jane Lord walked in ahead of him. She'd thrown a lumber jacket on over her shirt

and jeans; the broad white ribbon in her hair was
badly wrinkled now, and she looked very tired and
cross. The hideously functional appearance of the
room did not seem to impress her, but she blinked
against the lights and waited near the entrance until Kennedy gave her a chair. The mortuary manager waddled over and performed the introductions
rather distantly.

"I didn't realize you had a right to disinter the
body of my uncle without my permission," she
observed resentfully.

Hogan reached in his pocket and held out a folded
document to her. She peered uncertainly at its crisp
lettering and gave it back to him. "A court order,"
she said, half irritated, half surprised. "Whatever
for? Will you please tell me what is wrong?"

The bearded little doctor smiled his twinkling little smile. "Are you a nurse, Miss Lord?"

"Not registered. I never finished at the hospital—
the Continental Airways people offered me a job.
What does that have to do with it?"

"You clearly understand the nature of your uncle's cause of death?"

"Of course I do," she said impatiently. "It was
explained to me by Dr. Foreman, but I knew about
it anyway. A lump of marrow from his broken leg
got to his lungs and spread into the tissue, suf-
focating him. It happens all the time, and it's a
frightful business, but there was nothing I could do.
Surely you have no grounds to question Dr. Foreman's diagnosis?"

"Strictly speaking, no," he told her, just as chip-
per as a sparrow on the threshing floor. "And I
might add, Miss Lord, that Dr. Foreman left this
room about an hour ago, after he'd worked with me

all night. We proved that Mr. Bundy died from what was incontestably a pulmonary lipoid, and we agreed that Dr. Foreman was entirely justified in signing the certificate, since he had every reason to assume his patient's fracture must have been responsible."

"Are you implying. . . ." she began, but he held up his hand to stop her short. "Let me explain," he said. "You probably recall, Miss Lord, that we can make a microsection of the tissue, stained with osmic acid, which will show up fatty cells in black. This has been done, of course, and the resulting slide was quite characteristically positive. However, there's another test, of which you may not be aware. A second section, stained with gentian violet, should have revealed the immature red and white corpuscles that are invariably present in the marrow oil. That test was negative, Miss Lord; we made it twenty times. And I believe that the lieutenant and the sergeant want to ask you why."

Hogan stood over her, hands in his pockets, feet apart. His clear blue baby eyes were cynically disapproving, but he sounded almost unconcerned. "You got the right to remain silent, ma'am," he said and casually reeled the rest of the Miranda warning off to her in that half-scornful, half-complacent monotone most cops seem to fall into when they're set for you.

"I don't know what you're talking about," she said irritably. "Why should I get an attorney? You can't seriously mean to tell me you're arresting me or anything."

Joe Kennedy asked conversationally, "On Thursday morning, did you give your uncle an injection, ma'am?"

She sat up very straight and tense, and looked him squarely in the face. "Why do you ask me that? If Dr. Foreman has been here, he must have told you that he had prescribed a daily dose of calcium gluconate."

"Yes, ma'am, we found the puncture in the elbow vein. We figure it was milk you put into the hypo, not that calcium stuff for healing bones. You want to say so now or wait for us to prove it to the jury later on?"

The mortuary manager released a sigh and turned away. I glanced at Kennedy, who leaned against the tilework, studying the tip of his cigar. The bearded little coroner said chipperly, "Make no mistake, Miss Lord, the polarizing microscope at U.S.C. will tell us, if you won't. We can take pictures of the crystal pattern, and we'll see if it was milk, or olive oil, or three-in-one. A student nurse would know that any of them could be used to kill a man in less than fifteen minutes, if injected intravenously."

She stared at him, as carefully composed as if he'd propositioned her. She was the coolest number I had come across since I was twelve years old and visiting the carnival that had this girl who posed without a stitch of clothes on, from the inside of a block of ice.

"Why would I do a silly thing like that?"

"For money, ma'am," said Hogan, just as mildly as a priest. "You wanted to get married, and your boyfriend didn't make enough to pay the rent. We figure him and you are in this up to here."

I whispered into Suzy's ear and pointed at the phone extension on a table in the window bay. Jane Lord was saying scornfully, "What money, please, Lieutenant? I agree with you we should have money while we can enjoy the privilege. But Uncle Jerry didn't have much money, you'll find out, and most of it he left to Vera—Miss Carstairs, his former wife. I know he did, because he told me so himself. And if you talk to Bill, I think you'll soon decide he doesn't even understand. Bill is just kind and sweet and handsome and I love him very much, but he would no more hurt a fly. . . ."

The bearded little doctor winked at us, put on his hat and overcoat, and strutted off. I said, "Miss Lord, we know what you were interested in. We found the jewels in your beach bag, where you'd parked it in the shower stall. Four men have died for them, of which your uncle was the first. You should have realized that killing him was just like opening the lid of a Pandora's box. As long as he kept on his feet he could control the situation, but the minute he went down there were too many people waiting who had tickets for the show. You two were pretty clever, but you didn't really have a chance."

She looked at me as if I should go back to school. "If there was anything of value in my beach bag, someone put it there," she said. "At least a dozen people must have had the opportunity last night."

I shook my head, took Hogan's arm and drew him off into the window bay, where Suzy was just putting down the phone. "You haven't got a case," I told him soberly.

"That right? I figure we can break 'em down."

"It might take weeks, and they'll be out tomorrow on a writ. Listen, we've seen these two in action. You don't understand just what you're up against. The only real witness you've got left is Max the Dude. He saw what happened Tuesday night;

he followed them around and must have grabbed an
earful of their conversation, or he couldn't have
been sure of where the bundle was. He was so sure
of that, he even could afford to wait until last night
after the beach crowd would have left. But Max is
not the singing type, and if he were, his testimony
would be worth about two cents.''

"But darling, we can prove in court she killed
him!" Suzy pointed out, upset with me.

"Well, what about it? We can't prove it was in-
tentional. She'll simply claim she got mixed up
somehow and made a terrible mistake. It'll look
funny, but the chances are they'd have to let her
off. And there's no way of implicating him, of
course.''

Hogan jacked up his bushy brows for me. "We'll
take a crack at that right now," he promised me.

"You want a full confession, Dave?" I asked.
"From both of them? I think I know how it can be
arranged.''

He listened to me tell him how; the grooves
around his grimly weathered mouth pretended to
be shocked. ''We don't do business that way.''

"You won't be doing anything. I'll set it up for
you.''

He shrugged and jerked his grizzled head at Kennedy, who wandered over to us, lent a glumly
unreceptive ear and shrugged in turn.

Jane Lord was watching us from where she sat
across the room, still self-possessed and rigid on a
chair against the wall, a few feet from the door.
Hogan stalked out past her into the anteroom. The
mortuary manager left on his heels, and we trooped
after him while Kennedy stayed at the window to
commune with his cigar. I held the door for Suzy,

leaving it ajar behind me for an inch: not far enough to see, but more than far enough to hear.

The anteroom was small, and furnished only with a leather couch, two armchairs and a smoking stand. Two deputies in khaki uniform lounged in the doorway to the hall. The boy McHugh was sitting on the couch, still in his shorts and sweater, looking sleepy and relaxed. His wavy, golden yellow hair was only slightly mussed; his classically chiseled features and his Roman gladiator's body seemed absurdly youthful, wholly out of place. Hogan confronted him in grim-faced silence for a while. "Somebody put a pair of pants on him," he said at last. "This ain't the Hollywood Athletic Club."

The mortuary manager surveyed the boy's lean hips with something of a practiced eye and waddled to a closet in the wall. The boy stared at the suit of cheap blue serge, flushed to his ears and slowly climbed into the trousers, turned his back on us to zipper up. They were at least a foot too short for him; when he sat down again, the change in his apearance was from statuesque to hulking and uncouth. Hogan inspected him with cynical contempt.

"How old are you?" he snapped.

"Twenty-four."

"Listen, you, get this straight. I'm a lieutenant of detectives. Guys like you call me Lieutenant, or they call me sir. Where do you live?"

"At the Westminster . . . sir."

"That right? Nice place. Your folks got an apartment there?"

"No, sir, they're up in Bakersfield."

"You got a job?"

"I sell TV sets and appliances at Shultz and Kemp."

"*Lieutenant.*"

"Sir."

"How much you make?"

The boy flushed pink again under his tan. "I'm on commission, sir."

"Do better than six-seven hundred bucks a month?"

"No, sir, I don't."

"How much you paying on your car?"

"About three hundred dollars, sir."

"Where was you at last Tuesday night from midnight on?"

I gave myself a cigarette. Suzy removed it from my lips and wandered off with it toward the single window that supplied a view of the marquee. The mortuary manager was mumbling an excuse and waddling out into the hall; the deputies in uniform moved hurriedly aside to let him pass. The boy McHugh said cheerfully, "I was at home, in bed, Lieutenant, sir."

"That right? How come your girl friend says you was out in the backyard of her uncle's place?"

The boy jerked up his head, looked Hogan squarely in the face. He showed his perfect teeth in what amounted to a slyly foolish grin. "She couldn't have," he said. "Not Janie, sir."

"Oh, couldn't she? She told us it was your idea. She claims you talked her into this, and then you lost your moxie and forgot to finish him. That way she had to do the job herself on Thursday morning, and we got the goods on her from the post-mortem evidence. She don't like she should take the rap alone for what you planned, and leave you making whoopee with some other babe that can afford to set you up with an apartment and a car. Suppose you pass the gravy, punk."

I said, "Look, Bill, you're being had. We understand you're really not to blame. She simply told
you to be out there on the terrace, tie a string across
the steps and break a windowpane before you ran
away. For all we know, she may not even have explained. You were in love with her and you depended on her; she could make you do most anything.
She did the bad stuff all herself, like hiding Mr.
Bundy's flashlight, and like running down those
steps ahead of him, so he would have to follow her
and break his neck. Then when he only broke a leg,
she couldn't bring herself to knock him off right
there—it takes a lot less nerve to use a hypodermic
needle than it takes to use a rock. There's nothing
you can do to help her anymore, but you can help
yourself by coming clean. It's the Lieutenant's aim
to make you realize that, and to get a statement
from you for your own protection, don't you see?"

Suzy turned from the window, nodded to us,
dropped her cigarette into the smoking stand. The
boy had kept his crafty grin intact; we'd made
about as much impression on him as a circus act
would make on a Chinese philosopher. "Get him,"
said Hogan grimly. "In one head and out the other.
Maybe we should leave him have a little privacy, so
he can use 'em both." He gestured at the deputies
in uniform. "You fellows wait outside," he ordered
them, and stalked back into the autopsy room, leaving the door slightly ajar again.

I followed Suzy out into the hall and down the
stairway to the lobby with the carved Italian reception desk. A single bulb was burning in the chande-
lier; a smaller one in a reflector lighted "Joseph
Counsels Pharaoh" with sinister effect. Vera
Carstairs stood waiting for us at the desk. For three
o'clock on Sunday morning she looked positively

devastating in a streamlined tailor-made of fuchsia gaberdine and a gay Parisian scarf to keep the night air off her short-cropped yellow curls.

The smile she had for us was mostly war paint, but her languid drawl was cordial enough. "Am I in time? You asked me to dress up, you know."

"Just right," I told her, and performed the introductions.

Suzy said, "This is an awful imposition on you, Miss Carstairs. But we felt sure you'd want to help."

"Sit down, please, Miss Carstairs," I said. "You'd better brace yourself. We've got a very nasty job for you, but first we'll have to tell you things that will disturb you greatly, I'm afraid."

She sat in the receptionist's chair and let me hit her with the story, never interrupting me or showing more reaction than occasionally closing down her sharp, executive-blue eyes. When I had finished she said calmly, "Is that all of it?"

"As much of it as you'd be interested in," I said.

"Thank you. I think I understand." She sounded brittle now, although the war-paint smile was still on tap. "Of course I never knew, but Jerry had me wondering for years. I left his bed and board because I sensed he led some kind of double life."

"When you went down to see him Wednesday night, he didn't mention that he'd run across the terrace after Jane?" I asked.

"He was quite fond of her," she said. "She was his only living relative. He'd never have suspected her, but I suppose he mostly didn't want to tell me any more than he could help." She sighed and rose, as gracefully as if this were a social function of some consequence. "Shall we go up?"

The deputies in khaki hurriedly came to attention and stopped chewing gum when we approached them in the hall. They listened to me pretty doubt-fully, thumbs hooked in cartridge belts. They were big men themselves, with solemn, weathered faces and the spreading rumps made by patrol-car seats.

"What's your opinion, Jim?"

"If the lieutenant said so, it's okay, I guess." The deputy called Jim opened the anteroom and stuck his head inside. "You got a lady here that wants to see you, Mac," he barked.

Vera Carstairs swept past him in a cloud of Chanel Number Five. She left the door wide open, and the strident fervor in her cool soprano bounced back through the hall. "Oh, *Bill*! Sweetie, what have they *done* to you! Those awful clothes. . . ." From where we stood, we could just watch her pouncing on him, and the blank bewilderment clouding his face as he attempted to evade her on the couch. She pinned him to it in a flurry of fuchsia and perfume, more securely than a wrestler could have pinned him to the mat. "But this is simply *terrible*! Just wait until I see those stupid officers who dragged my baby into this!"

He managed finally to make himself be heard. "How'd you find out? Why are you here?"

"Sweetie, it's on the *radio*! They had a special bulletin at two o'clock. I couldn't sleep, so I was listening, and then I called the sheriff's office and they told me where you were. Of course I had to give them hell, but when they understood at last. . . . You see, my love, I *knew* you couldn't *possibly* have been involved." She shifted to a stagy whisper, and the knife went in so smoothly he still looked bewildered when the hilt fetched up against his ribs. "I told them that you were with me that night. It was the least I could do after what we *have* been to each other....."

From the autopsy room there came a sudden sound of scuffling and a scream of shrill hysteria before the door slammed shut.

THE EARLY AFTERNOON SUN cast a spiky shadow pattern from the avocado tree across our patio. It struck bright sparks of auburn gold from Suzy's hair while she poured coffee and arranged the breakfast set.

The dog sprawled on the tiles beside her with his massive tawny head posed on the cushions of her deck chair. Frank Brownell absentmindedly reached out to rub his sharply pointed yellow ears. The phony fifty-thousand-dollar check was burning in the ashtray, swiftly crumbling into wispy flakes. Its forger heaved a sigh of comfort and profound relief.

"You realize I didn't sleep a wink all night?" he grumbled for us. "If you hadn't told me it would save your client's life.... Hey, Johnny, what became of him? Where'd he fit into this?"

I stopped a forkload of fresh scrambled eggs in midair. "Now that's a good question, Frank," I said.

"You mean to tell me you don't *know*?" His indignation sounded almost comical. "You let them take that harmless little lush from right under your nose and lock him up somewhere, or maybe even knock him off, and you're not *doing* anything about it yet?"

Lieutenant David Hogan's elderly black Ford sedan came growling up the hill from Sunset Boule-

vard and parked across our driveway, on the wrong
side of the street. Its owner wandered up the lawn
and dropped into a chair between us, made selec-
tion of a strip of bacon, started gnawing on it,
threw another piece at Khan, who had been watching him expectantly. He pushed his hat back on his
grizzled hair and looked us over with a jaded eye.
"All over but the paperwork," he wearily announced.

"It does seem such a shame," said Suzy brightly.
"Dave, they are so young and healthy, and they
looked to be such normal children, didn't they?"

"Yeah, normal," Hogan said. "As normal as them
high-school kids we had a couple years ago that
blew her parents out of bed with twenty sticks of
dynamite. The way this Bundy case turns out, it
happens I was right. It was that Tarzan guy you
figured for a dumbo planned it all. The nurse just
fell for him like crazy and she let him talk her into
it. We got a couple of psychiatrists that's working
out on her right now."

"Put Frank out of his misery, Dave, will you,
please?" I said. "He's worrying about my hundred-
dollar client getting lost. The one he tricked me into
taking on."

Hogan supplied me with a heavy-lidded stare.

"You don't mean Cockeyed Artie Weil?" he
asked me carelessly. "He's in the county jail. A couple of the boys that's working this convention of a
bunch of jerks in bedsheets put the pinch on him at
his hotel. I would of told you sooner, but I figured
you might get your feelings hurt."

Frank almost swallowed his cigar. "You telling us
that fellow was a crook?" he yelped.

"A shakedown grifter," Hogan said. "He always

poses as a member of the family, and takes his score off people that inherit money that he figures comes a little hot. Sometimes he hires a private dick to check the lay. I spotted him from your description right away.''

"You put a lot of body English on it, Dave," I said. "That bow tie with the polka dots was pretty cute."

He sipped his coffee rather noisily. His craggy leather face was blankly innocent. "I was a little understaffed, and you can always use a buck. How'd you catch on?"

"Oh, Max had dyed his hair," I said. "You didn't know that, so you sent a dark-haired deputy who matched the photographs. And I remembered that your office issues Texas plates sometimes to your detective cars for undercover work. Only by then it was too late for me to call your bluff, you shifty mick. Next time you want to use me for a stalking horse, you might at least give me a chance to bill the county for my services."

Suzy remarked uneasily, "You know, somehow I wonder, Johnny, if that hunch of yours about this case was so far off. I mean about the eerie sort of way we were pulled into it, as if it had all been arranged...."

"Arranged for you to get your freezer, honey lamb," I said, and reached across the breakfast tray to pick a toast crumb off one corner of her pretty lips.

Don't miss these exciting **Raven House Mysteries**

---

41 DEATH AUDIT James A. Howard
Keeping a company in the black is a very sound business procedure. It can also mean a lot of grief...when murder is the key to balancing the books.

42 MURDER IN FOCUS Robert Julian
He was photographing on location and had a very tight schedule. He hadn't counted on being interrupted by a murder investigation...and making room in his schedule for an appointment with death.

43 THE NIGHTINGALE TRIVET Russell Mead
It was just an innocent piece of antique bric-a-brac, nothing that could possibly bring anyone harm—until it fell into the hands of a ruthless murderer.

44 DARK HOUSE, DARK ROAD Carter Wick
He was a successful moviemaker until it suddenly looked as if his newest production would also be his last—with a very real bullet providing the most ultimate ending of all.

46 RUN FROM NIGHTMARE Maxine O'Callaghan
She made a habit of keeping bad company at very strange hours. She was a girl who was looking for trouble — and trouble was exactly what she found!

47 CLUTTERKILL Gary Paulsen
A sniper was loose on the Chicago strip. He struck from rooftops, swiftly and at random — a man who loved death, and who killed for the sheer joy of watching his victims die.

48 THEY LOVE NOT POISON Sara Woods
Did the murderer live in the present? Or was she the reincarnation of a seventeenth-century witch who had killed in her own time, and had every reason to repeat her deadly game 300 years later?

Watch for these titles at your favorite bookstore.

RAVEN HOUSE MYSTERIES
are more than ordinary
reading entertainment.

Don't miss this exciting opportunity to read, FREE,
some of the very best in crime fiction.
It's a chance you can't afford to let pass by.

As a RAVEN HOUSE subscriber you will receive every month
4 thrilling new mystery novels, all written by authors who
know how to keep you in suspense till the very last page.
You may cancel your subscription whenever you wish.
Should you decide to stop your order, just let us know
and we'll cancel all further shipments.

CLIP AND MAIL THIS COUPON TODAY!